6/19/16

DAVID BADDIEL

Illustrated by Jim Field

HARPER

An Imprint of HarperCollins*Publishers*

To Ezra and Dolly, with particular thanks to Ez
for giving me the idea in the first place...

SUNDAY

CHAPTER ONE

Barry Bennett was always very upset at being called Barry. It was a stupid name for a modern nine- (nearly ten-) year-old boy. All his friends were called things like Jake and Lukas and Taj.

In fact, they weren't called things like that, they were called *exactly* that. Jake was his best friend, Lukas was his second best, and Taj was his third. Although sometimes that order was reversed and Taj was first. But, either way, none of them were called anything like Barry. Barry didn't even *know* anyone called anything like Barry. He didn't know, for example, anyone called Brian. Or Colin. Or Derek. Or any other name that no boy had been called since 1953.

Being called Barry was just one—although it was pretty near the top of the list—of the many things Barry blamed his parents (*Susan* and *Geoff*: go figure . . .) for.

Here, in fact, is that list, which Barry kept hidden under the pillow on his bed (a bed that *didn't*, by the way, have the fantastic Lionel Messi duvet on it that Lukas had):

THINGS I BLAME MY PARENTS FOR

1. Being boring.
2. Calling me Barry. (You see—told you it was near the top of the list.)

3. Being tired all the time.

4. Not letting me play video games.

5. Not buying me any video games. Or a Lionel Messi duvet.

6. Being REALLY, REALLY, REALLY strict. Examples: making me go to bed at 8:30 when all my friends stay up MUCH later; not letting me eat any sour Haribos in case they give me a tummy ache; and saying, "That's a swear," when all I've done is say BUTT, which isn't even a proper swear.

7. Being always <u>much</u> nicer to ~~my twin sisters~~ TSE than to me, just because they're a pair of Goody Two-shoes.

8. Not being glamorous or famous or all the things that the grown-ups in Mom's magazines are. (**Barry realized after he'd written this that it was a bit similar to Number 1, but he'd already started the list when he got to this point, and had**

written in pen, not pencil, so didn't want to cross it out and start again.)

9. Being poor. (Barry felt a bit bad about writing this one as he did sort of know it wasn't his parents' fault. His dad worked in IKEA, checking the flat-packed stuff into the warehouses or something, and his mom was an elementary school assistant. So he knew that meant they didn't earn very much. But he did think that if only they had more money then a fair amount of issues 1 to 8—although not being called Barry—would probably not apply.)

10. NOT EVER MAKING MY BIRTHDAY REALLY GOOD.

This was the biggest thing. All his friends had had their tenth birthdays recently, and all of them had been fantastic. Jake had had a go-kart party. Lukas had had a bowling party. And Taj had had a limo!

They'd all gone in it to the cinema to see the latest James Bond film!

Barry loved James Bond. It was partly why he hated being called Barry, as he knew that James Bond would never have been called that. I mean, he knew James Bond's name was James, but even if it hadn't been it would probably have been John or David or Michael. Or—as Jake often pointed out—Jake. Barry said this wasn't true, although in his heart he knew it kind of was, what with Jake being, in name terms, really quite like James.

Sometimes, Jake would even raise one eyebrow—which Barry, try as he might, just couldn't do: both of them always went up at once—and say, "The name's Bond. Jake Bond."

Barry agreed, without saying so, that it sounded kind of OK. Certainly better than, "The name's Bond. Barry Bond."

*

Jake (and his eyebrow) were at Barry's house on that Sunday, six days before his birthday, when Barry got really annoyed with his mom and dad.

All three of Barry's best friends were on the doorstep, listening to Geoff Bennett say, "No, sorry," which, Barry thought and not for the first time, was something his dad said a *lot*.

Jake was holding a Nike Premier League soccer ball, Lukas had on a pair of black Converse sneakers, and Taj was wearing a brand-new, this-season Chelsea top. Which made Barry feel, in his discount-store jeans and discount-store top and discount-store shoes, a bit terrible. Although not terrible enough to stop him wanting to go out and play with them.

"Dad," said Barry, "it'll only be for half an hour!"

"No, sorry," said his dad again. "You know we don't let you go in the park without a grown-up. . . ."

Barry looked back at his father's frowning face. He looked very tired, although Barry couldn't work out how tired, as Geoff Bennett always looked tired these days. There were bits of gray in his hair. In fact, it would be more accurate to say there were bits of black in his hair, because most of it was now gray. He was wearing his navy IKEA shirt, which he didn't have to on weekends. Barry wished he wouldn't, especially in front of his friends. Every time he'd seen them, Jake's dad had been wearing a smart suit, Taj's a leather jacket, and Lukas's dad—who, some of the time, played in a band!—skinny jeans and sunglasses (even, Barry noticed, when it wasn't sunny).

"But . . . ," said Barry, indicating with his hand the three boys on the doorstep, "all my friends are allowed to!"

"Well, that's up to *their* moms and dads, I'm afraid."

Barry turned and looked at his friends. At which point, Jake raised one eyebrow. Which gave his face an expression that seemed to say, very clearly, "Oh dear, Barry—such a shame that you're lumbered

with these silly, strict (and tired, bad-clothes-wearing) parents. . . ."

He didn't say this, though. He just said: "Sorry,

Barry," and turned around, bouncing the soccer ball as he went.

"Yeah, sorry, Barry," said Taj, joining Jake.

"Me too. Sorry . . . ," said Lukas, who for some reason waited until he'd got to the end of the Bennetts' front path before turning around again to say, "Barry."

And even though Barry knew that it was good to feel sorry for some people, like starving children on the sad bits of the news, he found that he really, really didn't like it that his friends were feeling sorry for *him*.

CHAPTER TWO

But that was just the start of Barry's bad day. It got worse later, when he was trying to talk to his dad during tea.

". . . So I thought maybe on my birthday—next Saturday—when I wake up, it would be good if waiting outside was an Aston Martin DB6 . . . ," Barry was saying, in between forkfuls of Asda low-sugar, low-salt baked beans on baked potato.

"An Aston Martin! Write that down, Ginny!"

"I'm writing it down, Kay!"

Barry carried on looking at his dad. He had chosen not to recognize his younger twin sisters. Barry often snuck a glance at his dad's *Daily* or *Sunday Express*, as he knew that James Bond would have to be aware of when dangerous stuff was happening in the world, and he had read that some countries did this to other ones. He had read that Iran, for example, did not recognize Israel, calling it instead—his dad had read this phrase out for him—the Zionist entity. Which made it sound all villainous, like Spectre (the secret world-controlling gang in James Bond). So, similarly, he did not call his eight-year-old twin sisters Ginny and Kay, but The Sisterly Entity. Or TSE for short.

He did, however, out of the corner of his eye, catch them doing that sarcastic thing they did, where one of them—Barry didn't like separating TSE into two, as that was kind of recognizing that they existed, but if he had to, he would refer to them as Sisterly Entities One and Two—would pretend to write down something he said, as if it was really important. Which of course was their way of saying that it wasn't important at all. Barry really hated it when they did that.

". . . So, Dad, on *our* birthday can you take us somewhere in a *Rolls-Royce*? Which you can keep in the garage next to the Aston Martin!" said Sisterly Entity One.

"Ha-ha-ha!" laughed Sisterly Entity Two, who was still running her index finger across her palm as part of the pretending-to-write-down-stupid-stuff-Barry-says mime.

"Yes, well, they're not *that* expensive to rent. I checked online," said Barry, trying as much as possible not to look at them. "And then maybe you can have, like, a tuxedo ready for me to wear and a cake with 007 on it, and all my friends can come dressed as Bond villains, and maybe you can have the film soundtrack playing, and you, Dad, can be Q, showing me gadgets, like a jet pack and a pen that's actually a gun, and—"

"Sorry, Barry, what?" His dad put down his *Sunday Express.*

"Weren't you listening? *Da-ad!*"

"Barry, please don't say Dad like that."

"Like what?"

"Like when you give it two syllables. And go right down on the second one. On the *-ad.*" This was Barry's mom speaking.

Barry looked over, but couldn't see her because, as usual, she was speaking from behind the dishwasher. As far as Barry could tell, Susan Bennett spent her whole nonworking life either loading or unloading the dishwasher. Days would go by when he never saw her, but only heard her voice, in between the clanking of plates and saucepans.

"I don't do that!" said Barry.

"Yeah, *Mo-om!*" chorused The Sisterly Entity.

Barry's mom and dad both laughed at that. His dad did that laugh which was also half a cough, and Barry could hear his mom's high-pitched giggle.

"Don't laugh at that!" said Barry, annoyed at having to acknowledge something said by The Sisterly Entity. "It's not even funny!"

"It was *quite* funny," said his mom, still not coming up from behind the dishwasher. All Barry could see, in fact, was her collection of egg timers—she had them in every color of the rainbow—sitting above the dishwasher on the kitchen counter. "You do make me laugh, you two girls . . ."

"Excuse me!" said Barry, feeling like he wanted to stamp his foot, but couldn't because his feet still didn't quite stretch to the floor from his chair. "Did anyone hear what I was saying at all?"

"Write that down, Ginny!"

"Well, I would, Kay, but I couldn't actually hear anything . . ."

"Oh yes, you're right. I thought I heard someone say something, but it must just have been the garbage men shouting in the street!"

Barry pulled a face at The Sisterly Entity. Then felt annoyed at himself as he realized that this meant that he was, in effect, recognizing them. But it still made him feel better. Until Sisterly Entity One said:

"Write that face down, Ginny!"

"I'm . . . a . . . really . . . stupid . . . looking . . . boy . . . ," said Sisterly Entity Two, moving her finger slowly across her palm.

CHAPTER THREE

Having broken his resolution never to recognize The Sisterly Entity, Barry thought he might as well kick them under the table. (His feet, being free-floating, were well placed for this.)

The last time Barry had kicked his sisters he had lost his pocket money for the week. But, seeing as that was only 75 pence, he reckoned it was just about worth it, and he had actually swung his feet back, in readiness to swing them forward toward their dainty little shins, when his dad said:

"Were you talking about your birthday party again?"

Barry let his feet swing back to their midway point. "Yes!"

"Oh, OK. Well, it's all sorted."

Barry's heart lifted at this. His dad was really going to organize the car and the casino and the gadgets and everything?

Geoff smiled at him, revealing his yellow bottom teeth, and bent down to rummage in his IKEA bag (one of those enormous blue ones made out of, as far as Barry could make out, a tent: his dad always had one to hand). "I was going to save this as a surprise for the day, but you've forced it out of me. . . ."

He sat up again, holding a DVD with the title: *Casino Royale.*

"What's that?" said Barry.

"What do you mean what's that? It's a James

Bond film. One of the most famous. Come on, Barry, I thought *you* of all people would know that."

His dad handed it over. On the front cover was a man with a pencil-thin moustache who sort of looked like James Bond, but not one Barry had ever seen before. It wasn't Sean Connery, or Roger Moore, or George Lazenby, or Timothy Dalton, or Pierce Brosnan. And it especially *wasn't* Daniel Craig. Who Barry *knew* was in *Casino Royale*.

"And I'm not just going to put it in the DVD player. We've got a projector at work that I can borrow and we can project it on to the living-room wall. That's probably white enough if we shut the curtains really tight—although they never close completely in that room, do they, Susan? Oh well, it'll probably be all right. Anyway, I thought that would be a great thing to do at your party. . . ."

Barry looked up. "What? That's it?"

"Huh?"

"No casino? Or car? Or tuxedo? Or gadgets?"

"Susan, what's he on about?"

"*I knew* it! *I knew* you weren't listening!"

"Barry, calm down . . . ," said his mom.

"*And* this isn't even the proper *Casino Royale!*"

His dad frowned. "It isn't?"

"No." Barry turned it around, reading off the back. "'An all-star cast spoofs the James Bond films in this hilarious 1960s comedy!! 007 has never been so funny!' It's a joke version! It makes fun of the whole thing!"

"Oh, Geoff," said Barry's mom. "You haven't gone and got the one with David Niven in it?"

"I don't know, Susan! I just went for the cheaper one on Amazon!"

"Da—" said Barry, and then realized he'd started to do the two-syllable thing again. Seeing The Sisterly Entity looking at him eagerly, as if willing him to do it, Barry made a fatal mistake. Which was to just repeat the first syllable again.

". . . Da," he said.

"I beg your pardon?" said TSE One, grinning madly. "Did you say . . . Da-Da?"

"I think he *did*, Ginny!" said TSE Two. "He said Da-Da. Like a baby. Like a baby trying to say its first words. To its da-da!"

"I didn't! I didn't! Shut up shut up shut up!"

"Barry, don't tell your sisters to shut up!" said his mom sharply. Still no sign of her head above the dishwasher, though.

"Does Diddums want his dummy from his da-da!?"

"Or does he want Da-Da to change his Nap-Nap?!"

"OK, Ginny. Kay. That's enough," said Geoff, although not very strictly, and like he was trying not to smile. "But Barry, that's enough complaining too."

"No it isn't! I hate you!"

"Oh, do you?"

"Yes! And Mom!"

And suddenly a feeling that had been welling up inside Barry for . . . well, since his dad had closed the door on Jake and Taj and Lukas just before tea, but in another way for much longer than that, maybe ever since he'd understood that, unfortunately, his name was Barry—a feeling that he wanted to both cry and shout and break something all at the same time—exploded out of him.

"I hate you because you're boring! And tired ALL THE TIME! And always TELLING ME OFF FOR NOTHING! And saying, 'That's a swear,' when all I've done is say BUTT!"

"Barry. That's a swear!" said his mom.

"NO IT ISN'T! And because you're so much nicer to THEM . . ." He pointed at TSE. They both grinned at the same time. ". . . than to ME! And because . . ." Barry realized by now that he was doing the list in his bedroom. He decided to miss out Numbers 8

and 9—"Not being glamorous" and "Being poor"—
since even in his rage he knew that they might just
sound a bit too horrible out loud. Especially as
loud as he was speaking now. "And . . . YOU NEVER,
EVER MAKE MY BIRTHDAY REALLY GOOD!!"

There was a short pause after he shouted this.
Then Sisterly Entity One said:

"Write that down, Ginny."

"I'm writing it down, Kay."

"Right," said Barry's dad. "Well, if that's how you
feel, we won't have a screening of *Casino Royale* on
your birthday!"

"GREAT!" shouted Barry and he threw the DVD
across the room. It spun around in the air as it made
its way toward the sink area. Barry was secretly quite
proud of the throw; his wrist had flicked sharply
as he'd released the disc, like an Olympic discus
champion.

"BARRY!!" his dad shouted. So loudly that, for

the first time this dinner time, Barry's mom looked up from the dishwasher. Just in time to be hit in the eye by a copy of *Casino Royale*, starring David Niven.

"OW!" she said, falling backward and out of sight again. Barry heard a bump; then one of the egg timers, the red one, fell off the kitchen counter and smashed.

Uh-oh, he thought.

"RIGHT, BARRY, THAT'S IT! GO TO YOUR ROOM!" said his dad, pointing upstairs—stupidly, really, as Barry knew the way.

"ALL RIGHT I WILL!" Barry shouted back. And because he was a little frightened by now, he ran out of the kitchen as fast as he could, swerving at the last minute to avoid the bits of glass and sand from the egg timer, which were sprinkled all over the floor.

CHAPTER FOUR

Barry lay in his bed, fuming. He'd gone straight to his room, without cleaning his teeth or anything, and slammed the door. But it had just come back at him as his door didn't really shut properly unless you closed it carefully, jiggling the handle up as you did it. So he'd had to do that after his slam, which felt completely at odds with a show of rage.

He lay there in his onesie—a zebra one, with ears and a tail, which was too big for him because it had been passed down from Lukas—and stared at his room. His head hurt. He wasn't sure why that was, but he'd read in another part of the *Sunday Express* once that stress brought on headaches, and he knew that he was very stressed at the moment.

It wasn't that easy to sleep in his room at the best of times as the Bennetts lived on a main road called the A41, and Barry's room faced it. The Sisterly Entity had, of course, been given the quieter room at the back facing the garden, which was BIGGER as well: some rubbish about them needing to have the bigger room because there were two of them. Barry did not recognize this.

As each vehicle went past, it would light up a different section of Barry's room, depending on which way it was going.

A car driving down the road would light up his wardrobe, or DEJN NORDESBRUKK as it had been called in IKEA.

A car driving *up* the road would illuminate the ceiling and the browny-yellow patch of damp immediately above Barry's bed, which he sometimes pretended was a map of Russia that he had to study for a secret mission.

A car turning into the road from the other side would throw a sweep of white light across the far wall, which had a James Bond poster on it— Daniel Craig in a tuxedo—and another poster, of FC Barcelona, which was a couple of years out of date but still had Lionel Messi sitting in the front row. Barry had always liked the way that both of his heroes stared out of the posters with intense eyes: Lionel like he was ready to go and beat eleven players single-handedly and score with a back-heel chip, and James Bond like he was ready to kill someone.

Every so often, his bed would shake as a truck went by.

But today he wasn't trying to get to sleep anyway. He was too angry. And he knew that if he went to sleep, by tomorrow the argument would all be forgotten about, and he didn't want that. He had meant it. In his anger, he had come to a deep and important realization: *his parents just weren't very good parents.* It made him sad to have this thought—his tummy fell as the words appeared in his mind, like it sometimes did when he was scared—but another part of him felt brave: like he was facing up to something.

"I wish I had better parents . . . ," he whispered. He could feel, as he said it, a tiny tear squeeze out of his left eye. It blurred his vision, making the damp patch look less like a map of Russia and more like a smear of poo. This got in the way of his train of thought a little. It was very distracting, the idea of someone somehow getting their bottom on the ceiling to plop upside down, and so, to get back into the moment, he repeated, slightly more loudly: "I wish I had better parents."

Then, from underneath his pillow, he grabbed the list he'd secretly written down of all the things that made his mom and dad a bit awful at their basic job of being his mom and dad. He held it up above his face and said, a third time, the loudest so far: *"I wish I had better parents!"*

And then suddenly the entire room started to shake.

CHAPTER FIVE

The walls were shaking like crazy; it was as if Barry's bedroom had a really bad fever.

The windows rattled and his little Aston Martin DB6 model car fell off the shelf behind his bed. Barry had never been in an earthquake, but he had seen them on the TV, and thought this must be what they were like. He clutched his duvet (MYSA ROSØNGLIM, white) in fear, frightened that maybe this was happening because of what he'd just said out loud.

He was about to say, "I'm sorry, I'm sorry, I didn't mean it!" He didn't quite know who this was addressed to—his parents, even though they weren't in the room, or, he supposed, God—but then he realized, *Oh, of course: it's a truck.*

He sat up.

It must be a very big truck, he thought as the room continued to shake. *It must have really powerful headlights as well,* he thought next as the far wall, the one with the posters on it, began to glow. What was odd about this glow, though, was that—unlike what usually happened when a truck or a big car turned on to the road, which was that its headlights would light up the whole wall as the vehicle moved past—only the area around his posters seemed to be glowing.

And the glow wasn't moving. Nor was it fading.

If anything, it was getting *brighter.* Maybe the truck had stopped outside the house? Barry did notice that the shaking seemed to have died down. But you weren't allowed to stop on the A41.

As he continued to look at the posters, a very strange thing happened. Lionel Messi's and James Bond's stares seemed to turn toward him. Like they were looking at him.

And then an even stranger thing happened.

Lionel Messi said: "Barry! Hey!"

Lionel didn't move from his sitting position, in between Iniesta and David Villa (see: told you it was out of date), with his hands on his knees. But his mouth did move. Definitely.

Barry, shocked and frightened, said nothing. But, through the shock and fear, he was also very, very curious. So he didn't look away.

"Eh! El Barrito!" said Lionel. "*Ven aquí! Rápido!*"

"He means come over here. Quickly," said another voice. A voice Barry recognized.

Barry moved his eyes sideways. James Bond was in exactly the same position he always was, but he had, quite clearly, raised his left eyebrow.

"He does?" said Barry hoarsely.

"Yes. I speak Spanish," replied James Bond. "And French, and German, and Italian, and Mandarin, and a smattering of Portuguese. Should be better, but y'know: very little action in Portugal."

". . . Right," said Barry, who by now was wondering if he should just start screaming.

James Bond raised his other eyebrow. Something that Jake couldn't do. "So?"

"So . . . what?"

"So come over here! Like he says! Otherwise

I might just have to shoot you. . . ."

Barry gulped. He thought it best to go along with it. So he got out of bed and walked toward the glowing wall.

CHAPTER SIX

As he approached the wall with the posters on it, Barry kept a close eye on Bond and, more importantly, on the Walther PPK with silencer now aimed at his chest. Barry could feel the too-big feet of his onesie dragging across the carpet (BJORNO MASTERLIGN): it was the only familiar feeling about this whole thing.

He walked toward the 007 poster, but James Bond flicked his cold, suspicious eyes to the right, so Barry moved over to where Lionel was smiling at him.

"Eh! Barrito! *Me recuerdas al niño en el avión en ese anuncio que hice!*"

"Pardon me?"

"He says you remind him of the little boy on the airplane in that advertisement he did," said James Bond. "You remember, the one with the basketball guy and the ice cream and stuff. God, Lionel, *why* did you do that? It's not like you don't earn a million pounds a minute as it is."

"*Estás celoso!*"

"I am not jealous. I do my work for the love of my country. And the ladies, of course."

"Er . . . hello?" said Barry. "I think you wanted . . . to talk . . . to me . . . ?"

"*Sí!*" said Lionel.

"Oh, speak English for crying out loud, Messi. You've played against John Terry. You must have at least learned some swear words."

"*Culo.*"

"That's not a swear."

Barry looked at Lionel, who tutted, but then looked back at him and said, in a strong accent, "Barry. Would you mind pleeze to stand in between me and the guy dressed like a waiter?"

"I am not dressed like a waiter! What waiter has a gun?!"

Barry shuffled across. "Here?"

"Yes, nearly. Just a beet to the left," said Lionel.

Barry shuffled a bit more. Now he was precisely in between the two posters. "Yes, good. *Espléndido!* Now shut your eyes and say the thing again."

"What thing?" said Barry. He dug his hands into his pockets (the onesie had quite deep ones), which was something he always did when asked a question he wasn't sure how to answer. In the corner of his mind he noticed that, crumpled up in his left-hand pocket, was the list of things that he blamed his parents for.

"Oh, you know the thing. What is it? Is hard for me in English. Remind me, 003 and a half."

"Seven! You know it's seven!"

"Yes, but on that poster you are a leetle half-size version of yourself! So 003 and a half! Ha-ha-ha! You see, Barrito, what I did there! Ees clever, no?"

James Bond raised his eyes to heaven. "Can we *please* get this over with? In two hours I have to be strapped to the underside of a stealth bomber."

"What thing?" said Barry again.

"Pardon?"

"What thing am I meant to say?"

"Oh. The thing about your mom and dad. Your wish."

"Oh right," said Barry. He shut his eyes.

"Loudly. Like you did last time."

"OK," said Barry. "Ahem." He didn't know why he

said that. It just felt appropriate. *"I wish I had better parents."* He opened his eyes. "Why? Why do I have to say tha—"

He was stopped from finishing the question by noticing that both Lionel and James Bond were waving at him. Little waves: like good-bye ones.

Barry frowned.

Then the glow behind the posters got super-strong, and the wall vanished in a huge burst of white light.

MONDAY

CHAPTER ONE

When Barry's eyes recovered from the shock, he couldn't see his room anymore. In fact, he wasn't *in* his room anymore. Nor was he in his house. Nor was it nighttime. The only thing that was the same was that he was still wearing his zebra-print onesie.

He was walking up some steps. He didn't know why he was walking up them. He felt scared, but something stopped him from doing what he would normally do when frightened: crying out for his mom and dad. He simply kept on going.

Just before he got to the top, Barry felt a fluttering by his feet. Looking down, he saw a creased, colored bit of paper, half-trodden into the step: a map. Barry bent down, peeled the pages off the concrete, and unfolded it.

The map was brightly colored and showed a city marked out with cartoon drawings of all the most important places, like the ones Barry had seen held by tourists on the odd occasions when he and his family would go to London. The city seemed to be called, as far as he could make out from the name written at the top, *Youngdon*.

Geographically, it looked a little like a map of London. The drawings showed all the big buildings in the same places, except instead of the Houses of Parliament there was something that looked like a cross between the Houses of Parliament and a soft-play center, called the Playhouses of Parliament. (It included a clock called Little Ben.) Hyde Park was called Hide-and-Seek Park, Nelson's Column was entitled Nelson-the-Bully-From-the-Simpsons Column, and both Oxford and Piccadilly Circuses appeared to be actual circuses.

In the middle of the map, though, there was a large, official-looking building that didn't match anything from the *real* London, above which was written, in big red capitals, three letters:

TPA

Barry looked up. While examining the map, he'd moved up a couple of steps and now he could see that he'd reached the top of a subway, looking out on to a street. It was a very busy street, in what looked like the center of a big city. There were shops, and tall buildings, and traffic, and more shops, and more tall buildings, and more traffic.

YOUNGDON

FA

YOUNGDON
BRIDGE

CANARY WHARF

POTATO MODERN

RIVER THEMES

LOO BRIDGE

SHARD
SKELTER

Barry was, frankly, disappointed. He knew he had come here by magic. And he reckoned that if you went somewhere by magic then it should be—well—a *really* different world, where people drove floating cars, or monsters spoke to you in computer code. Or maybe—and the map *had* led him to think this might be the case—it would be a world where everything was designed for children: where sweets grew on trees and Xboxes fell from the sky.

Here, though, all he could see were lots of grown-ups doing their boring, grown-up stuff: going to work, shopping, speaking very seriously on their mobile phones about money and offices.

Barry decided, therefore, that he had simply been transported to a big city he didn't know, perhaps one off the A41. As such, he thought it would be best if he just went home. He didn't know how to get home, though, so he shouted, at the top of his voice: "EXCUSE ME!"

It came out very loudly. Quite a lot of the grown-ups stopped what they were doing and looked at him.

"I'M BARRY AND I'M TEN YEARS OLD," he said. "WELL, NEARLY TEN. IN FIVE DAYS. AND I'M HERE ON MY OWN. CAN SOMEONE PLEASE HELP ME?"

Barry expected that, by shouting this, he would make at least one of the grown-ups come over and take him to a police station, or phone his parents or something. But *one* of the grown-ups didn't come over. They *all* came over. At once.

There were loads of them, crowding around him. Couples mainly: fat couples, thin couples, old couples, young couples, hairy couples, bald couples (even the women), well-dressed couples, couples who both wore slacks, smelly couples, couples who weren't easy to describe one way or another. They were all saying things.

"Barry!" they were mostly saying at first. "Barry!"

"Yes?!" said Barry to some of them, before realizing it would take too long to answer everybody.

"Barry!"

"We'd be great for you!"

"You'd love it at our house!"

"Come and be with us, Barry!"

And others were saying: "Here! Please! Have a look at this!"

"Take our card!"

"Here's our CV!! Would you mind just reading it? Take your time!"

While they were saying these things, they were trying to hand him bits of paper or cards. On the bits of paper were photos of the couples, looking smart and smiling. There was also lots of information about each couple—where they lived and what kind of car they owned and how much money they earned and stuff like that—but Barry didn't have time to read one to the end before another was thrust into his hand.

"Hey! OK! Thank you, but I just need to get back to my house!"

"No, Barry! Come and live with us at our house!"

"No, *our* house is much nicer!"

"We live next door to a theme park!"

"Our house is made of cotton candy!"

"That's not true!"

"OK, it isn't, but we've got a lot of cotton candy under the stairs!!"

"What?" Barry said. "Why are you saying all this?"

They were all around him, bumping him and knocking him in their desperation to get him to look at their bits of paper. He was starting to feel afraid. Then, suddenly, he heard a voice, a kid's voice. Which made him realize, for the first time, that he hadn't seen any other children on this street, or in this crowd. The voice was tinny and amplified.

"OK, get back," said the voice. "Come on! All of you! Back we go!" It sounded strangely familiar. "You know the procedure!"

The adults all fell silent, moving away from Barry, who squinted and saw, coming across the crowd, two figures he immediately recognized. One of them was talking through a megaphone.

Barry stared at them. "Lukas!" he said. "Taj! What are you doing here?"

CHAPTER TWO

"**S**orry, but we don't know who you're talking about," said Taj. "I am PC 890 and this is PC 891."

"PC?" Barry realized then that they were wearing uniforms. Not exactly like police uniforms—they were more, in fact, like dark blue . . . onesies—but similar enough for Barry to say: "Like Police Constable?"

Taj looked at him as if he was talking gibberish. "No! *Parent Controller*, of course!"

"Huh?" said Barry. "What's that?"

"Watch and learn," said Lukas. Which made Barry think that he definitely *was* Lukas as that was exactly the sort of thing he would have said.

Lukas and Taj turned around. Lukas raised the megaphone to his mouth again and Taj took out of his pocket a large silver whistle. Lukas looked at the crowd, who were still all standing there, waiting. "OK, everyone! Go back to your homes!" he said.

"But I'm on my way to work!" came a voice.

"Well . . . ," said Lukas, "all right. Go back . . . or onward . . . to your place of work! Whatever! You all know the procedure!"

"You said that before!"

"Yes, all right! Anyway. We will be taking this boy to the Agency. You are, of course, all welcome to send your applications there, those who aren't already on file. And now . . ."

He nodded to Taj, who blew on his whistle as loudly as he could. The blast was deafening and went on for quite a long time. Barry put his fingers in his ears. The crowd began to move silently away. Well, Barry thought it was silently; as he had his fingers in his ears, it was hard to tell. So he took his fingers out. In fact, the grown-ups were all murmuring.

"I'll get our updated file sent in straight away. . . ."

"He'd be perfect for us. . . ."

"Stupid PCs, always turning up from nowhere . . ."

When they had finally all gone, Barry turned to Taj and Lukas. "Do you really not know that your names are Taj and Lukas?" he said.

"PC 890," said Taj.

"PC 891," said Lukas. "And now, if you don't mind . . . ?" He paused, doing a questioning face. Barry knew what the question was, although it made no sense that Lukas—his best friend, or his best friend sometimes—was asking it.

"Barry," said Barry.

"Really? It's really Barry?"

"Yes, of course it is! You know that!"

"And you're really about to be ten? In five days?"

"Yes," said Barry, "you know that too!"

Lukas turned to Taj and shook his head as if they couldn't understand what Barry was talking about. Taj frowned and looked concerned. About what, Barry had no idea.

"OK, Barry," said Taj. "Would you please . . . follow us?"

They took the tube from a station called Green Booger Park. Barry sat in between PC 890 and PC 891. Every so often he would notice a grown-up in the seat opposite look over at him meaningfully. One mouthed at him something that looked like, "Pocket money: we're talking *three* figures." Another, as she was getting off, tried to slip him a card, but PC 890—Taj—flicked her away.

They got off at another station called Ha-Ha-Ha This Station Is Called Watery Loo. (The name took up the entire wall along the platform.) When they came out, standing in front of them was a large, important-looking building, like the ones Barry had seen on a school trip to Downing Street once. (They hadn't gone into Downing Street, just looked at it through the gates, while Mr. Podmore, their teacher, had read something out from the internet about it.) Around the building were a lot more grown-ups, some of them just standing there, others sitting by tents or lying in sleeping bags. They looked up expectantly when they saw Barry.

Lukas got his megaphone back out.

"Move away, please!"

The grown-ups looked disappointed, shuffling backward to let them through. The three boys walked up to the door, which was large and black and on which was written, in big brass capitals:

TPA

Barry stepped back and looked again at the building. It looked exactly like the drawing at the center of
the map of Youngdon he had found on the subway
steps. Except, of course, much bigger.

Lukas knocked on the door. It was opened by a
girl in an orange onesie, with dog ears.

"Hello, 890 and 891. Stray, is it?"

"Yes."

"Through you go . . ."

Inside was not a grand hallway, as Barry had
imagined, but a very, very busy office, with lots of
people working there. By people, I mean children:
all the workers seemed to be about Barry's age. He
and Lukas and Taj walked through them. They were
all wearing orange onesies—although some had cat
ears, and some bunny ones, as well as the standard
dog version that the girl who answered the door
had been wearing. Some of them were carrying
files; some were talking; some were at desks on

computers. Others seemed to be having meetings.

Barry, Lukas, and Taj carried on walking.

"Where are we *going*?" said Barry.

"To the Head," said Lukas. "That's the proper procedure when we find a stray."

"A stray?" said Barry, remembering that the girl at the entrance had used the same word.

"Yes," said Lukas. "A stray kid."

By now, they had reached a big oak door. A plaque on it read: TPA HEAD. Lukas knocked.

"Come in," said a posh, stern-sounding voice.

CHAPTER THREE

Lukas opened the door into another office. It was plush, with wood panels and a thick rug. At the other end of the room was a big wooden desk.

Behind this desk sat Jake. He was wearing a black onesie, with a built-in shirt-and-tie pattern, and no ears.

"Ah, 890 and 891. This would be the stray, I believe?" His voice sounded nothing like it normally did. He normally said "innit" a lot. Now he sounded fancier than someone out of *Downton Abbey*.

"Yes, sir."

"Splendid."

"Thank you, sir."

Taj and Lukas started to back out of the door.

"Hang on, where are you going?" said Barry.

"Done our job. And, besides, we have to be home for tea," said Taj.

"Home for tea with who?" said Barry.

Taj looked at him like he was mad. "Our parents, of course." He shut the door.

Barry looked over at Jake.

"Do sit down," said Jake, gesturing to a chair on the other side of the desk. On the desk was an antique wooden box and some kind of machine with buttons and a microphone. "Your name again is . . . ?"

"Barry. It's Barry. You know it's Barry!" He sat down, feeling, by now, quite frustrated and annoyed.

"Yes, I should know. But when they told me I

didn't quite believe it. We've never had one called that before, you see."

"Right. And I suppose your name isn't Jake?"

Jake raised one eyebrow, just like Jake always did, which only made it more infuriating when he said: "I'm just known as the Head, I'm afraid."

"The Head of what?"

Jake gave a big sweep of his arm. "This. The Parent Agency." He opened the antique wooden box. "Sour Haribo?"

Barry looked down. Jake—or the Head as Barry was indeed starting to think of him—had taken out of the box a pink-and-green sweet, the type that are circular but also have a point.

"Thanks," Barry said, taking it and popping it into his mouth. He very much wanted to know what the Parent Agency was, but halted for a moment to savor the sourness, before it dissolved to just being an ordinary sweet.

"Do you really not know how it works here?" said the Head.

Barry shook his head.

"Oh, I see. Sometimes that happens with strays. Memory loss, et cetera."

"No, I haven't lost my memory. I come from another place—a place that *you're* in."

"I am?"

"Yes. Where you're just my friend at school. You don't work in an office or anything. And grown-ups have children, and they live with them. They don't . . . do whatever it is they were doing when . . ." Barry struggled to remember their numbers. " . . . PCs 890 and 891 found me."

"Well, never mind," said the Head, in a way that suggested that Barry was, of course, deluded, but there was no point in trying to tell him that. It reminded Barry of how his dad was sometimes with his grandpa, who had an old person's disease that meant he couldn't remember anything. "The way things are in *this* place, which is the real place everybody lives in, is that grown-ups don't"—and here he mimed quotation marks—" 'have' children, whatever that means. Here, children choose their parents."

"Choose . . . ?"

"Yes, of course. A childhood is far too important to just randomly let grown-ups"—he did the mime again—" 'have' children. No. What we do here is work with children who have yet to choose their parents, like yourself—you're nine, yes?"

Barry bristled at this. "Nearly ten. In five days."

The Head's eyebrow went up. It actually went up even farther than it usually did, the top disappearing somewhere under his hairline. "Oh my God!" he said, instantly hitting a button on the machine in front of him, and bending his face down to the microphone. "Secretaries! We have a Code Yellow,

Orange, Green, Blue, and Red!!"

Barry sat up in his chair. He'd begun, while listening to the Head, to like the sound of this world. But he didn't like the sound of that. And he liked even less the *sight*, coming through the door of the office, of The Sisterly Entity.

CHAPTER FOUR

Barry was about to refuse to even look at TSE, and certainly not listen to them, but it very quickly became clear that, in this world, even The Sisterly Entity were not quite the same as they were in his world.

To begin with, like everyone who worked at the Parent Agency, they were wearing onesies, which they would never have done at home. Plus their hair had gone *weird*: it had been combed up, a bit like their granny's hair used to be in black-and-white photos. And, crucially, they were looking at him—Barry—not like they were about to make fun of him, or tell on him to Mom or Dad, but as if he was really, really important.

One reason Barry felt this was because it was actually quite hard for them to look at him. They had come in sideways, carrying a large silver tray, but were still turning their heads as far as they could toward him, and smiling politely. On the tray were five very large egg timers. They were made of glass and each one was a different color: yellow, orange, green, blue, and red. The Sisterly Entity set the tray down on the Head's desk, between him and Barry, and went to sit on two chairs at the side of the room.

Then they took out, from the pockets of their onesies, notepads. Real pads—they both flicked them open—followed by real pencils, sharpened and ready to write. Neither of them was getting ready to mime with their palm.

Not wanting to look at them, Barry said to the Head: "Those are very big egg timers."

"Egg timers? These, Barry, are Hourglasses."

"Oh yes, I've heard them called that too."

"These are 24-Hourglasses. Dayglasses," said the Head. "So. Five dayglasses. And in five days' time . . ." He picked up the first glass, the yellow one, and dramatically—a bit overdramatically, Barry thought—turned it upside down so that the sand started to fall and said, ". . . you, Barry, will be ten!"

"Yes," said TSE One. "Hardly any time to make sure he doesn't end up . . ." She trailed off.

"You know . . . ," said TSE Two, also trailing off.

The Head did a small, quick, and supposedly-but-actually-not-very-secretive headshake at them. Barry knew this was body language for "Shhh, don't tell him about *that*."

"Hold on!" said Barry. "What happens to me if I don't find . . ."—he could hardly believe he was saying it—". . . um, parents . . . by my tenth birthday?"

"As you can see, Barry," said the Head, ignoring the question again, "the sand in the 24-Hourglass trickles down very slowly. It will take, in fact, exactly . . ."

"Twenty-four hours?" said Barry.

"Yes," said the Head, looking a little put out, since—

Barry now realized—he had only been pausing for effect, and had wanted to say that himself.

"So! Secretaries!" said the Head, moving on. "What would you suggest? In terms of parent-finding?"

They frowned. One turned to the other and started whispering furiously, while the other nodded furiously, and went "hm," "yes," "right." Furiously. Then they turned back to Barry and the Head.

"We think, sir, that, given the . . . you know . . . circumstances . . . ," said TSE One.

"Yes, the . . . ," said TSE Two, glancing significantly at the row of Dayglasses, *"circumstances . . ."*

". . . the best thing might be our One-a-Day Parent Package Offer, which we could run for five days," said TSE One.

"We don't, as you know, sir, normally offer that for five days running, but in the *circumstances . . . ,*" said TSE Two.

"Can you please stop saying *circumstances* in that . . . that . . . whispery, looking-around-as-you-say-it way!" said Barry, breaking the rule of a lifetime—well, of the last month—by addressing The Sisterly Entity directly. Although he'd already started to think of them as The Secretary Entity.

"Interesting," said the Head. "I like it."

Barry looked at him. It was as if he hadn't spoken at all. He took a deep breath and decided, for the moment, to forget about his *circumstances*. "This . . . package," he said resignedly. "How does it work?"

"We'll match you with five different sets of parents," said Secretary One.

"And you can then try them out. A daily trial. Each set of parents for a day," said Secretary Two.

"And then . . . ," said the Head, "you can tell us which set you like best. And Bob's your uncle! Or rather your parents! Sorry, I shouldn't have said Bob's your uncle; that's confusing. Unless one of those parents did indeed have a brother called Bob, in which case Bob would indeed . . . be your uncle."

"Right . . . ," said Barry, confused.

"Also," said Secretary One, "if you let us know of anything you might want to do with each set of parents . . . go to the zoo, visit a theme park, a trip to the cinema . . . we can take a note of that now and let them know in advance!"

This, Barry had to admit, was starting to sound interesting.

CHAPTER FIVE

The Head took out, from under his desk, a gold laptop. "So . . . ," he said. "Let's begin by having a quick look at the profiles . . . ."

He opened the lid, pressed a button, and then turned the laptop around so Barry could see the screen. On it, a series of pages, a little like Facebook ones, were flicking past in a slide show.

"These are the Parent Profiles," said the Head. "Every prospective parent has to create one of these and send it in . . . ."

Barry could see, as the pages went by, photographs of grown-ups smiling, mostly posing outside their houses. Some of them stood in front of trampolines, or swimming pools, or big collections of toys. Others in front of tables laden with delicious-looking food.

"Each one includes a short filmed message too. . . ."

The Head clicked on a box on one of the pages. A couple in their front garden suddenly started moving. "Hello, I'm Sheila," said the woman.

"And I'm Michael!" said the man, who was holding a guitar. "And this is our song about us!"

"And hopefully . . . ," said the woman, pointing at camera, "*you* . . ."

Strum strum strum went Michael's guitar. "We are the Radcliffes," they sang cheerfully. "And we never have any bad tiffs! We like to go to parks and zoos. And our house . . ." At this point, they turned and gestured toward their front door. ". . . has seven loos!"

The Head clicked pause. "I don't like them much," said Barry.

"No," said the Head, doing, by his standards, quite a small eyebrow raise. "They seem a bit weird. But you get the general idea."

The slide show carried on, each new page showing a new set of parents with their photos. Then a page came up on which the photo of the parents was really blurry. Barry couldn't make out what these two looked like at all, although there was something familiar about them. But he didn't have much time to think about it as the Head turned the laptop away from him.

"So," said the Head. "That's just a few of the couples on our books. There's many more . . . ."

"And," said Secretary One, "as we said, if you let us know what you might want to do with each set of parents, we can inform them of your preferences."

"Oh . . . right," said Barry. This being a question

that he didn't quite know the answer to, he dug his hands in the pockets of his onesie. And felt, in the left-hand one, a piece of crumpled paper.

He took it out and unfolded it. It was the list of things that he blamed his parents for.

For a second, just seeing this familiar object made him feel homesick. But he put that feeling out of his mind quickly and looked at the list. It had suddenly become really useful.

The last item, Number 10—the one about his parents never making his birthday any good—gave him an idea. "Well, it's my birthday in five days' time," he said. "I was going to have a party. Maybe . . . maybe each set of parents could organize a . . . party?"

The Secretary Entity looked at each other, then at the Head.

"You want to have . . . five parties?" he said.

Barry nodded. The Head thought for a second, then shrugged and nodded back at The Secretary

Entity. On their pads The Secretary Entity started writing down a word. It seemed to be the same word, beginning with G. Barry frowned. G, he saw, R, E, E, D and what looked like the start of a Y, when the Head spoke again.

"So, Barry. Perhaps if you could tell us what kind of parents you'd like to have . . . ? Then we can begin."

The Secretary Entity turned a leaf together and looked up at Barry expectantly.

"Uh . . . ?" said Barry.

"Shoot," said the Head.

"Shoot what?" said Barry.

"Say what sort of parents you'd like. In an ideal world. Which this is."

Barry looked back down at his list. The first thing that caught his eye was Number 9, the one he had always felt most guilty about: "Being poor." He realized with a rush that this was a big problem, perhaps the biggest, with his parents. He looked up and saw The Secretary Entity with their pencils poised over their pads.

"Rich," he said. "I'd like to have rich parents."

"Write that down, Secretary Two," said Secretary One.

"I'm writing it down, Secretary One," said Secretary Two.

CHAPTER SIX

"**C**hampagne, sir?" said Lord Rader-Wellorff's butler.

Barry didn't quite know what to say. He was overwhelmed as it was, sitting in the back of a stretch Rolls-Royce. He hadn't even known such things existed until Lord Rader-Wellorff's chauffeur pulled up in it outside the Parent Agency.

"I don't think I'm allowed to drink champagne. I'm only nine," he said.

"Ha-ha-ha! This is special *children's* champagne, Barrington!" said Lady Rader-Wellorff, who was sitting at the other end of the stretchy bit of the car with Lord Rader-Wellorff.

Peevish (the butler) had filled their glasses and moved over to Barry, holding out the bottle and a glass on a silver tray. They had been driving for about an hour down a long road.

"Yaahs!" said Lord Rader-Wellorff, which Barry had realized by now was how he said "yes." "Château Bolly-Wolly-Doodle-All-the-Day 1993. Seven hundred pounds a bottle! Tastes of grapes, lemonade, and Sherbet Dib Dab!"

"All right then," said Barry. "Thank you . . . Peevish." Peevish bent his head toward him—well, his whole body in fact, as Peevish didn't seem to be allowed to sit down and so could only stand in the car by bending over—and filled his glass.

Lord and Lady Rader-Wellorff lifted their glasses toward Barry.

"Cheers!" they said.

"Cheers!" said Barry, raising his own glass. *This*, he thought, *is going to be* awesome.

It had all happened very quickly. Well, quite quickly. After Barry said the words "rich parents," the Head had smiled and nodded at The Secretary Entity, who were writing the words down. Then there was clearly a moment where no one quite knew what to do next; and suddenly the Head went, "Oh! Right!" and pressed another button on the machine in front of him and said: "Send up the Rader-Wellorffs!"

Then there was a second slightly awkward moment when no one said anything for a bit. The Head offered Barry another Sour Haribo from his box, but Barry knew that if he ate a lot of sour sweets in one go he'd get a tummy ache, so he said no. And everyone just sat in silence for four or five minutes.

Then there was a knock on the door and after that things *did* start happening very quickly. The Head stood up and said, "Come in!" and suddenly into the room burst a man in golf pants and a tweed jacket, holding a pipe, and a woman wearing a huge flowery dress with pearls and a wide-brimmed hat which had what looked like a model of an enormous country house perched jauntily on the top of it.

"This is the most exciting day of our lives!!" she said, and the two of them immediately circled around to give The Secretary Entity an enormous hug.

"No, er . . . Lord and Lady Rader-Wellorff," said the Head gently as The Secretary Entity began to look quite frightened. "Your one's over there. He's called Barry." He nodded his head toward Barry.

They looked over, confused.

"Bah-rie?" said Lord Rader-Wellorff.

"No, Barry."

They looked at each other. "Do you mean . . .
Barrington?" said Lady Rader-Wellorff.

"Er . . . Is that what Barry's short for, Barry?" said
the Head.

Barry sheepishly shook his head. "I don't think
so . . . ."

"Well, never mind!" said Lady Rader-Wellorff. "We
can always change it later. To Jeremy or something.
When you're . . . *our son*!!"

And then the faces of Lord and Lady Rader-Wellorff
broke into two very big smiles, which—considering
they both had very white, very protruding teeth, like
horses—nearly blinded Barry.

"This is the most exciting day of our lives!" said
Lady Rader-Wellorff, and they rushed over, circled
around him, and hugged.

As Barry downed the last drop of Château Bolly-
Wolly-Doodle-All-the-Day 1993, thinking, *Wow, it*

really does taste of grapes, lemonade, and Sherbet Dib Dab, the stretch Rolls turned off the main road and into a small village. A sign said *Bottomley Bottom*. In the middle of the village stood a huge pair of iron gates, which opened automatically as they approached.

"Would you like a better view of the house and grounds, sir?" said Peevish to Barry, following a wink from Lord Rader-Wellorff. Peevish was still bent over. It didn't look very comfortable, especially as he was wearing a black suit and tie with a high starchy collar. Barry rather wished he could ask him to sit down.

"Er . . . Yes, please."

Peevish whispered something to the chauffeur, who pressed a button near the steering wheel. Barry heard a smooth shushing noise above his head and felt a breeze ruffle his hair. He looked up. A rectangular panel in the roof of the car had opened, showing the clear blue sky above. Barry stood up and his top half was out of the car.

It was amazing. The car was traveling up a long gravel path, bounded on both sides by very tall pointy trees. Barry could feel the wind in his face. Then the Rolls turned out of the trees and up a little hill, to reveal a huge stately home, like ones Barry had only seen before on TV (and once when his family had gone on a day trip to Hatfield House, but then their car had broken down in the parking lot and they had had to stay there and wait for the tow truck to arrive, so he only saw it from a distance). And somewhere else . . . He had seen this house somewhere else. . . .

A second later, Lady Rader-Wellorff popped up beside him, smiling. "Welcome, Barrington, to Bottomley Hall!"

And then Barry realized where he had seen Bottomley Hall before. On Lady Rader-Wellorff's head. Or, to be more precise, on her hat, where the little model of it was presently trembling in front of his eyes as if a wizard had shrunk the real one to a

thousandth of its normal size.

"Yaahs!" said Lord Rader-Wellorff, sticking his head out of the roof too.

"Oh, that's better," said Peevish, whose head appeared last, as he groaned with relief and tried, in the small space left in the roof rectangle, to stretch his lower back.

CHAPTER SEVEN

"**P**leased to meet you, Mr. Barrington, sir. . . ."

"Delighted to make your acquaintance, young Master B."

"At your service, sir . . ."

When the car stopped, and Barry was let out by the chauffeur, a line of men and women was there to meet him. The women were all wearing white aprons and black dresses, and the men were all dressed in suits and ties and high collars, like Peevish.

"If there's anything I can do to make your stay more pleasant, Master . . ."

They were all murmuring things like that, really quietly. As Barry went past them, the men bowed and the women did a movement which involved crouching and bending their knees, like something he'd seen The Sisterly Entity do when they practiced their ballet.

"Thank you," said Barry to each of them. "Thank you very much."

"This is our staff, Barrington. Well, *your* staff now," said Lady Rader-Wellorff. She waved toward them as a group. "Cook, cleaner, pants folder, bath runner, personal booger collector, that sort of thing."

"Don't be silly, Lady R-W," said Lord Rader-Wellorff. "You know we had to fire the PBC." He turned to Barry. "Found him eating them on the sly."

Barry nodded, feeling a bit sick. He passed the

last two members of staff, a man and a woman, who were standing with their heads down.

"If you need anything at all, Barry . . . ," said the man in a familiar voice.

"Yes, Barry, anything . . . at any time," said the woman in an even more familiar voice.

They didn't look up. But there was something about them. In fact, they reminded Barry very much of the couple he had seen on the Parent Profiles at the Head's office, the blurry ones. Plus, Barry could tell, just from the way they spoke, that they really meant what they said, about being there if he needed anything. This made him feel strangely warm inside, and he was about to say, "Thank you very much," when suddenly Lady Rader-Wellorff grabbed his hand and started marching him toward the door of the house, up a series of steps. She moved her knees very far up and very far down as she walked, like Barry had seen horses do at the dressage in the Olympics. He tried to look back at the man and woman, but they just kept gazing at the ground.

Barry was shown to his room by Peevish. It took about half an hour to get there—up various enormous staircases, past hundreds of old paintings, through the West Wing and down the North Wing and around the corner of the Library.

His room was astonishing. It was, as far as Barry could make out, bigger than his entire house. In the middle was a four-poster bed, and from the windows, which were massive, you had a view of the gardens—which Peevish told him were over a hundred acres—and the Bottomley Hall lake.

Then Peevish asked Barry if he would like him to put his luggage away.

"I don't have any," said Barry.

Without even blinking, Peevish said: "No problem,

Your Eminence." (Peevish seemed to improvise quite a lot when it came to addressing Barry.) "We have a selection of clothes already in place for you." He opened a very big, ornate wooden wardrobe next to him.

Barry peered into the wardrobe. Hanging inside were about twenty black suits, a hundred shirts, some ties, and ten or so pairs of golf pants. Barry did not know what to say. Peevish took out one of the suits and held it up against him.

"All in your size, honorable Sir B. Specially tailored by Jackson, Jackson, Jackson, Jackson, and Jackson of Savile Row."

"The Jackson Five?" said Barry, who knew about them because his dad only listened to music from the 1970s.

Peevish looked at him as if he was a bit simple. "I suppose so, Your Heavenly Brightness."

Then Barry was taken to meet Lord and Lady

Rader-Wellorff again. He and Peevish stood outside the door of the dining room. Peevish knocked.

"Come!" barked Lord Rader-Wellorff's voice from inside.

There was a short pause.

Peevish frowned. "What, in?" he said.

There was another short pause.

"Yaahs, of course, you big idiot!" said Lord Rader-Wellorff. "It's time for Barrington to meet his new brothers and sisters!"

CHAPTER EIGHT

Peevish sighed and opened the door. Inside, Lord and Lady Rader-Wellorff were seated at the end of a very long table. Lady Rader-Wellorff still had a hat on, only now with what appeared to be a model of the garden and grounds, rather than the house, on it: there was even a small working fountain in the middle.

Also seated around the table were—Barry counted them quickly; he was good at math—eight other children, of varying ages, boys and girls, all wearing golf pants and tweed jackets, of varying sizes.

"Barrington!" said Lady Rader-Wellorff, leaping up and slightly sprinkling him with fountain splash. "Come and meet your brothers and sisters!"

"*Potential* brothers and sisters, Lady R-W . . . ," said Lord Rader-Wellorff. "Let's not jump the gun!"

"Fiddlesticks!" she replied. She came around and stood behind Barry, gently pushing him in the direction of the other children, who were all looking up at him. Most of them, it has to be said, in a not very friendly way. "Everybody! This is our new son— or soon will be, I'm sure—Barrington! Barrington, meet . . . Jeremy, Teremy, Meremy, Heremy,

Queremy, Smellemy, Sea Anemone, and Dave."

"Hello . . . ," said Barry.

"Hello . . . ," they all said back. Not, it has to be said again, in an especially friendly way.

Lady Rader-Wellorff was looking at the boy called Dave, a small thin child with glasses. "We really must get around to your name change, Dave. What do you think of . . . Bellamy?"

Dave didn't answer.

"Er . . . Lord Rader-Wellorff? Lady Rader-Wellorff?" said Barry.

"Please," said Lord Rader-Wellorff. "Call me Henry. George Tristram Forbes Benedict Louis Jerome Mumford St. Aubyn B'nard-B'nard Eugene. Rader-Wellorff."

"Yes, and please call me . . . ," said Lady Rader-Wellorff, ". . . Penelope. Virginia Phoebe Sienna Nigella Bubbles Daphne Clarissa Jemima Elizabeth B'nard-B'nard Virginia. Rader-Wellorff."

"Er . . . you said Virginia twice?" said Barry.

"Yes. I'm called it twice! What was your question?"

"Why . . . ," Barry continued, ". . . do you want to have more children if you've already got so many?"

Lady Rader-Wellorff and Lord Rader-Wellorff looked confused, as if this had never occurred to them before.

"Well! To be honest," said Lord Rader-Wellorff eventually, "I think, when the Agency asks children what kind of parents they want, quite a lot of them say, um . . ."

"Rich . . . ?" said Barry.

"Well . . . ," said Lady Rader-Wellorff, "we don't like to say. But yes."

"And . . . ," said Lord Rader-Wellorff, "some of our

lot are growing up—Jeremy, Queremy, and Meremy are almost ready to fly the coop!—so we really wanted a new young'un. Didn't we, Lady R-W?"

"We did, Lord R-W!" said Lady Rader-Wellorff. "So, Barrington, tell us about this *party* we're going to organize for you!"

CHAPTER NINE

In his bedroom, Barry looked at himself in the mirror. He wasn't, it has to be said, entirely comfortable in the suit. Peevish had helped him put it on, which had felt a little weird as his mom and dad hadn't helped him dress for a long time. But then again he didn't normally wear suits. And certainly not shirts with cuff links. And bow ties. Well, he had once worn a bow tie, to a party of Taj's, but it had been a clip-on.

The shirt even had a high stiff collar, like Peevish wore, which you had to tie the bow tie around. Barry had tried to tie the bow tie himself, thinking it couldn't be that different from the knot he tied in his laces, but it just meant that his neck ended up looking like a big shoe.

So Peevish helped him. And, even though he wasn't comfy, he looked good, Barry thought, surveying his image in the mirror once more. He looked a bit . . . a bit . . . like James Bond. Which was very good. As that was what the party was meant to be about.

It had been difficult to explain the party theme, as neither Lord nor Lady Rader-Wellorff nor any of the children with names like Jeremy had ever heard of James Bond.

It was becoming clear to Barry that this world, although very like his in some ways, was also quite different, and not just in the obvious children-choosing-their-parents way. But he had done his best to explain to his prospective mother and father about his spy hero. Although they'd been confused about a lot of things—MI6, Spectre, jet packs, and Barry going Dah Da-Da-Da/Dadada/ Dah!da-da-da/Da-Da-Da/DAH-DAH!/Dadada— they had jumped up in the air, clapping when he said two little magic words:

Casino.

And:

Guns.

"Oh!" said Lady Rader-Wellorff. "We've got *loads* of those!"

"Casinos?" said Barry.

"No! Guns. But we can do the casino in the Great Room, can't we, Lord R-W?"

"Yaahs," said Lord Rader-Wellorff. "As long as you don't lose another three million like you did last time, Lady R-W!! Ha-ha-ha!! Hmm? Hmm?!"

"Ha-ha-ha!"

Barry had laughed along with this, but then stopped, realizing he didn't actually know what he'd been laughing at.

There was a knock on the door. Barry thought about what to say. Then he remembered.

"Come!"

Silence. Then, from outside the door: "What, in?"

"Er . . . yes."

The door opened. Peevish leaned in. "Your guests are waiting for you, oh great Punjab," he said.

CHAPTER TEN

Barry had never seen anything like it.

The Great Room alone was bigger than his school assembly hall. It was lit by a series of enormous hanging chandeliers, whose light sparkled off the silver turning handles of three large roulette wheels, which had been set up in the middle, and off the jewelry of all the amazingly dressed ladies who were filling up the space beneath.

There were also loads of green tables, around

which some of these ladies—but mainly men in tuxedos—were sitting, playing cards. Everyone was holding drinks in tall glasses and talking and laughing. In the corner, a man in another tuxedo, only with a really long jacket, was playing a grand piano. It did look, Barry had to admit, very like some of the scenes in *Casino Royale* (the proper one, not the one with David Niven in it).

It even *sounded* a bit like it as the man on the piano was clearly trying very hard to play Dah Da-Da-Da/Dadada/Dah!da-da-da/Da-Da-Da/DAH-DAH!/Dadada. Only not getting it quite right.

Above the piano, strung between the walls, was a large banner—made, as far as Barry could make out, of silk—on which someone had managed, in the few hours since he had told Lord and Lady Rader-Wellorff the idea, to embroider the words BARRINGTON'S JAMES BOUND PARTY.

"Barrington!" screamed Lady Rader-Wellorff and

rushed over. She was wearing a long ball gown and a new hat, which had a model on it of what looked like a . . . stretch-limo sports car. "Do you like it?" she said, seeing Barry look up.

"Yes . . ."

"It's an Aston Martin. That's what you said James Blond drives, didn't you?"

"Bond . . . ," said Barry.

Lady Rader-Wellorff opened her arms and gave him an enormous hug, squeezing him tightly between her quite large bosoms. As she bent down, the stretch Aston Martin at the top of his vision wobbled.

"We will, my darling! We are!" she said.

"What?" said Barry, slightly muffled.

"Bonding! Of course! Drink?" She stood up again and snapped her fingers. Peevish appeared from nowhere, carrying a tray.

"Er . . . yes, please . . ."

"Peevish. Did you make up the drink as Barrington explained?"

"Without question, Lady Rader-Wellorff."

She took a triangular glass off the tray and handed it to Barry. "A martini. It's still lemonade with a grape in it, rather than vodka and an olive. But, as you requested, stirred, not shaken."

She smiled and Barry took the glass.

"Er . . . actually, I said it should be . . ." He paused and looked at her big smiling face. "No, right. Thanks very much." He took a sip of the drink, which was delicious.

"Chocolate?"

He looked up. Peevish was now holding a tray of golden balls, arranged as an enormous pyramid.

"My goodness, Peevish, with these you're really spoiling us . . . ," said Lady Rader-Wellorff.

Peevish smiled and bowed his head at her.

"No thanks," said Barry. "Maybe later . . ."

"What would you like to play? Blackjack, quoits, *feu-en-peu*, Texas Hold'em, Five Card Naughty Bum, Penny Come Quick, Tuckers Maltings, Burundu, Stinky Finger Nothings, or Lucky Dicky?"

"Um . . . I don't know any of these games."

"Oh," said Lady Rader-Wellorff, looking very disappointed. She thought for a moment. "Silky Knick-Knacks? Basically, the dealer is the flop, and each player has to lead with a jack, which is called the Hunter, and then you bet who's going to have the lowest suit in any one color as long as it's not diamonds. If it is, the flop removes his Silky Knick-Knacks—i.e., hands over his cards, of course—and . . ."

"No, I don't really . . . I don't think I can play that. Sorry."

"Hmm. What can you play?"

"Top Trumps," said Barry. "And Snap."

Lady Rader-Wellorff shook her head. "Frightfully

sorry, Barrington. Never heard of those."

Barry looked around. "I could play roulette. That looks like fun."

Lady Rader-Wellorff brightened immediately. "Super idea!" she said. "Here, have a chip!"

For a second, Barry expected to see her hand over a thin fried potato covered in salt and vinegar, but instead it was a small red plastic circle. On it were written the words: *One million pounds.*

She pressed it into his hand and began marching him in the direction of one of the roulette tables.

"Er . . . is this the smallest amount you have?" said Barry, looking at the chip.

"'Fraid so!" she said, without a backward glance.

CHAPTER ELEVEN

Lady Rader-Wellorff pulled Barry hard toward a particular roulette table, around which were seated Jeremy, Teremy, Meremy, Heremy, Queremy, Smellemy, Sea Anemone, and Dave.

"Hello, everyone!" she said. "Can I leave Barrington with you?" They all looked up. No one said anything. "Super!" said Lady Rader-Wellorff. And disappeared into the crowd.

Barry sat down in between Jeremy and Teremy.

There was hardly any room, and they didn't move up much to let him in.

"Place your bets, please."

Barry looked up. Peevish had appeared and was now wearing a weird cap with a transparent green peak. With a smooth smile, the butler twisted the roulette wheel and set the little white ball spinning around its edge.

Jeremy, Teremy, Meremy, Heremy, Queremy, Smellemy, Sea Anemone, and Dave all started frantically placing their chips on the squares laid out on the long green table. Jeremy on red, Teremy on black, Meremy on odd, Heremy on even, Queremy on the first twelve, Smellemy on the middle twelve, Sea Anemone on the last twelve, and Dave on a corner of the table that just had a tiny bit of cheese stuck to it.

"No bets, Your Massive Importance?" said Peevish. Barry realized he was talking to him.

"I don't know where to put it."

Peevish leaned over and looked Barry closely in the eye.

"I think twenty-three is always a good bet, Your Bigness." And then he winked.

"I don't know," said Barry. "I always like the number nineteen."

Peevish sighed. "No, Your Great Silliness. Twenty-three. That's the BEST BET."

"Oh!" said Barry. He looked at the ball, spinning around the edges of the wheel like a cyclist going around a velodrome at top speed. It started to fall down the ramp of the wheel, heading toward the numbers.

Quickly, he picked up his million-pound chip and, after a couple of seconds of frantically looking— where was it?! Oh yes, there between twenty-two and twenty-four—he put it down on twenty-three. Peevish, at that point, seemed to nod to himself, and . . . Barry wasn't sure, but he thought he *might* just have pressed something under the table.

At any rate, the wheel stopped spinning very suddenly and the little white ball bounced down from the edge, spun a bit on twenty-four, but then settled snugly into twenty-three.

"My goodness," said Peevish. "There's a surprise."

"Um . . . how much have I won?" said Barry.

Peevish sprinkled a series of one-million-pound chips on the table and pushed them toward him with a little shovel.

"Thirty-six million pounds, Your Richness."

"Oh my God," said Barry. He was about to leap up and stick both hands in the air, like he'd just scored a goal, but then he noticed that all the other children were staring angrily at him.

"That's not fair!" said Jeremy.

"You did it, Peevish!" said Queremy.

"The new child always wins!" said Meremy.

"*Waaaaaaaaaaaah!!!*" said Sea Anemone.

"Hmm, this is a lovely piece of cheese . . . ," said Dave.

"Um . . . sorry," said Barry, not sure what to do. Peevish had appeared beside him with a small plastic bucket, like you get on a beach.

"For your chips, Your Chipfulness . . . ," he said. And ladled them in.

"*Waaaaaaaaaaaaahh!!*" continued Sea Anemone.

"Look, I don't want to upset anyone . . . ," said Barry.

"Nonsense, Barrington!" said Lord Rader-Wellorff, bursting through the crowd around the table. "Jolly well done. And now: guns!"

CHAPTER TWELVE

Barry was very excited on the way to the shooting range. He imagined it would be something like the ones he'd seen in various James Bond films, when James Bond practiced his skills: a long indoor hall with, at the far end, a row of one-dimensional dummies with targets for faces. And at the other end would be somewhere you could shoot from, with a selection of handguns—Walther PPK? Colt M1911?—and some earmuffs for the noise.

He was so excited, in fact, that he said, "Are we there yet?" twice on the way. He had time to say this as it took a lot longer to get there than Barry had expected. Instead of the shooting range being, for example, in a secret chamber under the house, he and Lord Rader-Wellorff and all the other children had got into another stretch limo—this time a stretch Range Rover—and Peevish started driving them out into the countryside.

It wasn't all that comfortable a journey. His bucket of chips rattled against his leg all the way. Sea Anemone was *still* crying and all the others were looking at Barry as if they'd really prefer it if he wasn't there.

But Barry didn't care. He couldn't wait to start aiming at those dummies. *Bang!* Take that, Goldfinger! *Bang!* In your face, strange Spanish man with the blond wig from *Skyfall*! He even started thinking about some of the clever one-liners he might say after shooting them. "Suck on *that*, dummy!" *Ha-ha*, he thought, after he came up with that.

By the time they arrived, it was starting to get dark. Peevish got out of the car and went over to a small shed. He walked in and flicked a switch. Lights flooded the area they were standing in—which turned out to be not a long hall with dummies with target faces at one end, but a long muddy field. Peevish came out of the shed, holding a bundle of greeny-brown anoraks and flat caps.

"Put those on, children!" said Lord Rader-Wellorff, who, Barry noticed, was already wearing similar gear. The children all did as they were told. Then Peevish returned, pushing a wheelbarrow stacked up with what appeared to be a number of enormously long black trumpets. He started handing them out to the children one by one.

"What are these?" said Barry, when it was his turn.

"Guns, of course," said Lord Rader-Wellorff. "This model is our own personal family shotgun: the Rader-Wellorff Flintlock-Mechanism Blunderbuss. Bessie for short. Goes orff with quite a bang, though, so watch out!!"

Peevish handed Barry one of the Bessies. Barry immediately fell over. It was literally the heaviest thing he'd ever held.

"Ha-ha-ha-ha!!!" he heard one of the other children—it might have been Jeremy or Teremy or even Meremy—say as he struggled to get up. "Stupid Barrington's too weak to hold his own gun!!"

"I'm not! I just . . . Peevish, can you help me . . ."

"Certainly, Your Weakliness."

". . . slipped."

Barry managed, with help from Peevish, to stand back up. He put the gun to one side of him, leaned on it, and tried to look relaxed and jaunty.

"May I just…our Idiocy…?" said Peevish. Barry

frowned. Peevish adjusted Barry's flat cap, which had ended up backward on his head, so that it faced forward again.

"Thank you, Peevish," said Barry, wondering whether he should give him a chip from his bucket as a tip. But before he could do so, Lord Rader-Wellorff bellowed:

"Right!! Line up, everyone!"

The children—all of whom, apart from Barry, seemed to understand how to carry the Bessies so as not to fall over—lined up. Barry tried to make it look all right and perfectly normal that he was using his gun, basically, as a walking stick.

"Right, Peevish," shouted Lord Rader-Wellorff. "What's the target today?"

Peevish went back into the shed and came out again, holding not a dummy, not a cutout figure of a man with a scar and a monocle who may have been in charge of a criminal organization trying to take over the world, but a big silver platter with a big silver dome on it. He walked in front of the line of children, and said: "*Voilà!*"—which Barry thought was French for "Here you are!"—and took the big silver dome off the big silver platter.

Underneath was a large gray-and-white bird with beautiful yellow eyes and a black pointy beak. It looked terrified, shaking with fear. It flapped its wings, trying to fly away, but Barry could see that its legs were held to the silver platter by a series of silver chains.

"Perfect. The grouse are so big and flappy and . . . shootable this time of year, eh, Peevish?"

"Whatever you say, sir."

"All right. You know the drill."

Peevish put the silver dome back on top of the bird and walked about a hundred meters away from the line of children.

"Hoist!" shouted Lord Rader-Wellorff. All the

children heaved their Bessies up onto the top of their chests, pointing forward. With a supreme effort, Barry did so too, though he thought his arms were going to break.

"Aim!" shouted Lord Rader-Wellorff. All the children moved their guns toward Peevish. Barry, every muscle straining, did so too.

"Now! Remember! First shot goes to the new boy!"

"What?" said Barry, who had been very much hoping to pretend to shoot when the time came.

"Special treat. Special privilege."

"DA-AD!!" said Jeremy, Teremy, Meremy—oh, you know, all of them.

"Stop complaining. It was the same for you when you arrived. If he misses, one of you can bag the bird! So. Are you ready, young Barrington?"

"Um . . ."

"Splendid! Let her go, Peevish!"

With an extra flourish, the butler took off the silver dome again and expertly released the chains. The grouse flapped uncertainly, rising to just above Peevish's head. It looked like it had been held captive so long, it didn't understand where it should go.

"Come on, Barrington!" shouted Lord Rader-Wellorff.

"Go on, you stupid idiot!"

"Shoot, you dummy!"

"What are you doing? Kill it!!"

All this from the other children.

Barry didn't know what to do. He really, really, really didn't want to shoot a defenseless bird. So he said: "I don't want to!!"

CHAPTER THIRTEEN

"**W**hat's going on, Lord R-W?" said a shrill voice. It was Lady Rader-Wellorff, who had appeared through the bushes with a number of guests from the casino.

"Can't make it out, Lady R-W. Barrington doesn't seem to want to take his shot!"

"Doesn't want to? But I thought you said you liked guns?"

"I did, but . . ." Barry didn't know what to say.

His arms were killing him, and all these people were watching, and he could feel the other children smirking at him.

"Hmm. Not really a son of mine so far, it seems," said Lord Rader-Wellorff. "OK, Jeremy, Teremy, Meremy, Heremy, Queremy, Smellemy, Sea Anemone, and Dave: fill your boots!!"

Barry wasn't sure what that meant—most of them did have rain boots on, but they were full of their feet already—but it soon became clear that what it meant, basically, was *shoot the bird*!! Because they all started aiming very, very intently toward it. With every ounce of strength he had left, Barry then did something which, to be honest, he hadn't been expecting to do.

He stepped in front of the bird and shouted: "Put your guns down!!"

Everyone froze and looked confused. Barry could hear the flapping of the grouse above his head.

"Pardon, Barrington?" said Lady Rader-Wellorff.

"I said, put your guns down. Let the bird go!"

In Barry's mind, this sentence was meant to be accompanied by a smooth, James Bond–like move of the Bessie up to his shoulder, and then an even smoother sweep of it around in a semicircle, to protect the bird. Unfortunately, it was *actually* accompanied by him swinging the barrel up to his face, hitting himself on the chin, and falling over backward.

In fact, it would be truer to say that he went: "I said, put your guns down. Let the *birrfgggghowww!*"

The children all looked at each other. Slowly, Barry picked himself up from the ground, using the Bessie less as a gun and more as a crutch.

And then Jeremy swung his gun toward Barry and said, "Why should we do that?" At which point, all the other children swung their guns toward Barry as well.

"Children! No!" said Lady Rader-Wellorff.

"Now, now!" said Lord Rader-Wellorff.

"Oops . . . ," said Peevish.

But the guns of the other children remained trained on him. Barry felt the sweat breaking out on his forehead. He felt terrified and very, very tired, all at the same time, a combination he hadn't before known was possible. He looked over to the crowd of people watching and suddenly seemed to see the two servants—the man and woman, the ones with familiar voices—who had been standing by when he had arrived. They were looking at him with concern on their faces . . . their familiar faces. With concern. With hope. And with something else that Barry couldn't quite name.

He heard a click.

It was Jeremy, or rather, Jeremy's gun. Barry knew that time was running out. He felt something against his leg. He looked down. It was his bucket of chips: thirty-six million pounds' worth.

His legs, at least, had a tiny bit of strength left in them, so he kicked out—out and up, like Lionel Messi might have done when aiming for a free kick that needed to go up and over the wall—and the bucket rose above them all . . .

. . . turning over and over, almost in slow motion . . .

. . . and spilling thirty-six million pounds of chips into the air.

Immediately, Jeremy, Teremy, Meremy, Heremy, Queremy, Smellemy, Sea Anemone, and Dave dropped their guns and started rushing all over the field, arms outstretched, trying to catch the falling chips. As did all the guests and all the servants —apart from the oddly familiar two, who seemed to have vanished—and indeed Peevish.

The grouse—which suddenly seemed to understand what was best for it—opened its wings and flew away, high over the trees.

Barry looked around. Standing there, looking crestfallen, were Lord and Lady Rader-Wellorff.

"Hmm," said Lord Rader-Wellorff. "That didn't go quite according to plan, did it? Still. Anything else we can do for you, Barrington?"

"Yes," said Barry. "I'd like to go back to the Parent Agency, please."

TUESDAY

CHAPTER ONE

"**B**arry! Barry! Over here, Barry! Barry!" The voices came from all around him. Everywhere he looked there was another flash. It blinded him—there were so many cameras.

"Come on, Barry, don't look so surprised!" said Vlad Mitt. He tugged his arm—already around Barry's shoulder—tighter, pressing them together.

"One of you and the missus with Barry, Vlad?" shouted someone.

"Certainly. Come on, Morrissina . . . ."

Morrissina, Vlad's wife, came over and put her arm around Barry too, so that he was standing between them. She put her other hand on her hip and, for some reason, stuck out her leg so that her bare knee showed through her dress.

"Mitts and teeth!" she said. That was her catchphrase, which meant the three of them—the Mitts and Barry—should smile. He felt Morrissina and Vlad turn together and he felt them, or at least it seemed as though he felt them, smile. He couldn't help joining in; it was, after all, really, really exciting being at this film premiere, in the center of Youngdon, with the crowd shouting and all the photographers trying to get his picture. And so, as the cameras flashed again, he felt his lips spread wide apart and a great big smile fill his features.

*

On Barry's second meeting at the Parent Agency, the Head had been very apologetic about the Rader-Wellorffs.

"So sorry," he said. "It's odd, because we've placed quite a few children with them very successfully in the past."

"I know," said Barry. "Well, I know there's quite a few children there. I don't know how successful it is."

The Head raised his eyebrow; a big raise, leaving only a small amount of eyebrow hair visible below his bangs. He glanced over at The Secretary Entity, who shook their heads and looked at Barry as if he'd said something really inappropriate.

"Hmm. Well, if you say so. We haven't had any complaints before. Anyway, let's move on." He grabbed the second 24-Hourglass, the orange one, and turned it over. The sand began its slow trickle down, from top to bottom. "We have four days left before . . ."

"Before what?" said Barry. The Head had stopped speaking and started to look troubled.

"Before the end of your Five-Parent Package!" interjected Secretary One, much to—or at least it looked like this to Barry—the Head's relief.

"Yes! Exactly! So . . . Barry," said the Head. "What sort of parents would you like for your second day?" The Secretary Entity raised their pencils above their pads. Barry took the list out of his pocket again.

"What *is* that bit of paper you keep on looking at?" said Secretary One.

"Oh, it's just some thoughts I had written down. About the kind of parents I . . . don't want, I guess. So that I can make sure I don't choose them."

"Shouldn't we keep it in our files?" said Secretary Two.

"No thanks," said Barry, who suddenly felt very

protective of his list. He didn't quite know why. He scanned it. He'd covered Number 9—"Being poor"— with the Rader-Wellorffs. Number 1 was "Being boring." Interesting parents would be good . . . but then he remembered that he could kill two birds with one stone by going for Number 8: "Not being glamorous or famous."

Or, rather, the opposite of Number 8.

"Famous. I'd like to have famous parents."

"Great. No problem!" said the Head. "Famous parents always want loads of children, don't they?"

The Secretary Entity nodded earnestly as if the Head had said something very wise.

"Yes. But I'd like to have famous parents who *don't* already have any other children, please," said Barry. "It didn't really work out with . . . me and the other kids last time."

"Oh," said the Head. "Hmm. Let's see . . ." He took out the gold laptop and started flicking through profiles. "No...no...hmm...not this couple, they've already got one from every country in the world . . . Oh, there's that famous singer and his partner, but they have two and they *will* insist on dressing them in gold lamé suits, so . . ."—he looked up at Barry—". . . probably not for you."

Secretary One raised her hand. "Head, sir?"

"Yes, my dear?"

"What about Vlassorina?"

The Head slapped his forehead, and said: "I can't believe I hadn't thought of that!"

"I wrote it down earlier," said TSE One, showing the word VLASSORINA on her pad.

"So did I," said TSE Two. Although she was scribbling away furiously as she said it.

CHAPTER TWO

No one actually told Barry who Vlassorina was until he was picked up by a man in a Ferrari outside the Parent Agency five minutes later. The man was wearing a black suit and shades, and had an earpiece, with a little microphone in front of his mouth.

"Hi," he said as Barry got in.

It was a red Ferrari. Like the Rader-Wellorffs' stretch Rolls-Royce, it was a model that Barry, who knew a lot about cars, had never seen before, with pop-up headlights and millions of dials on the dashboard and a steering wheel covered in what looked like diamonds. You sat in it very low: Barry felt like his bottom was nearly on the tarmac.

"Name's Jonty. I work for Vlassorina." Then to his microphone: "Ready to roll."

"Hello," said Barry, who thought that Jonty reminded him of a younger and trendier Peevish.

"Roof off?" said Jonty, starting the car, and revving the accelerator. The engine sounded amazing, like some kind of monster clearing its throat. They sped off down the road.

"Um . . . OK," said Barry, who hadn't realized the car was a convertible.

Jonty pressed one of the many buttons on the dashboard. The roof didn't just go back with a slow whirr. It flew off, instantly, like a giant had flicked it off with an enormous finger.

"Oh!" said Barry.

"Good, isn't it?" said Jonty, raising his voice, since the roar of the engine was now five times as loud.

Barry looked around. The roof was crashing down the road behind them, turning over and over. Other cars swerved to avoid it. "But—"

"Oh, don't worry, Barry. Vlassorina has a deal with Ferrari. They just fit a new roof every time," said Jonty, pressing his foot down so hard on the accelerator that Barry was thrown back in his seat.

"Uh . . . what kind of person is Vlassorina?" shouted Barry, the noise now so loud it was like they were actually sitting inside the engine.

"Vlassorina, my friend, is two people!"

"Two people? What, like some kind of two-headed mutant?"

"Ha-ha-ha!" shouted Jonty. He swerved around a corner at top speed. "You're telling me you've really not heard of Vlad Mitt and Morrissina Padada?"

"Er . . . no . . . ," shouted Barry.

"Good grief. Get with it, Grandpa. They're only the coolest celebrity couple on the planet!"

"They are?"

"Yes!" The car suddenly braked, throwing Barry forward in his seat. They were at some traffic lights. "Haven't you seen any of Vlad's movies? *Black Smell*? *A Hundred Days Till Christmas*? *Froggie Goes A-Courting*? *Insta-Man*? *The Shuffling Tree*? *Fish and Chips: The Movie*? *Death in the Car*? *Death in the Car 2*? *Death in the Car . . .*"

"Er . . . three?" said Barry.

"No, four," said Jonty. "He wasn't in three. They got Jackie Noodle—you know, from the *Wonky Monkey* movies?—to play his part in that one. Vlad was furious."

"Oh," said Barry.

"He's also the face of *Stink-Bombe*." Jonty pronounced this in a very French way.

"His face is a stink bomb?"

"No. He's the *face* of *Stink-Bombe*. The smelliest perfume in the world. And Morrissina—she's a pop star!

You must have heard of her!"

Jonty was revving the accelerator pedal again as he spoke. The lights changed and they sped off. Barry had to hold on to the dashboard to control what felt like g-force on his face.

"No. Sorry . . . ," said Barry.

"You're kidding me. She used to be in *Girlish*! You know, who won *Talent Mess* two years ago? And then had a massive global hit with 'My Dog's Surprised by His Own Farts'?"

"That's a *song*?"

"Yes. You must know it!" Jonty opened his mouth wide and hit a much higher note than Barry would have guessed him able to. "He sleeps by the fire/When we watch the news/Then when one pops out/He looks confused!"

"Wow . . . ," said Barry.

"Yes, the record company was surprised by the choice of it as a single too. But it worked!! Number one in fifty-seven countries. And then there's the dance . . ."

"The My-Dog's-Surprised-by-His-Own-Farts dance?"

"Yes. You know, down in a heap pretending to be asleep, then up on all fours—surprised face! Then you move your face around, pretending to bark."

"Right."

"Morrissina's solo now, of course. And she used to be called Sally. But then she did a big deal with a supermarket and—anyway, they can tell you more about it themselves. 'Cause here we are!!"

Jonty pulled the car up to a gate. Not like the grand old gates at Bottomley Hall. It looked just like a very, very high white wall. Jonty pressed a button on the gate.

"Can I take your order, please?" said a voice.

"Two Big Burgers with triple fries and a choco-milk milkshake, please," said Jonty.

"Oh," said Barry, "I'm not that hungry. Although if they do chicken nuggets I wouldn't mind. . . ."

"Coming right up," said the voice.

"Sorry, Barry, that isn't an order," said Jonty, turning to him and winking again. "It's a code."

There was a whirring noise. And, as Barry looked ahead, the white wall slid slowly into the ground, revealing a very, very tall skyscraper. He looked up, up, up and up, and could just make out that the top of the building was shaped like an enormous letter V.

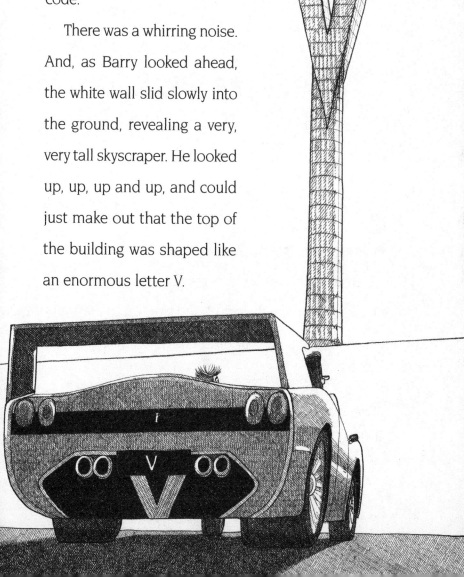

CHAPTER THREE

"**S**o . . . who else lives here?" said Barry as the elevator rose to the top floor, marked *P. House* on the elevator button. Barry knew that P stood for Pent, although a small part of him wanted to ask Jonty if it stood for Pee. He suppressed that with a giggle.

"No one," said Jonty.

"No one?" said Barry. "But it's an enormous building!"

"Yes," said Jonty. "Vlassorina wanted to live somewhere very high. But obviously not somewhere where they'd have to bump into *ordinary* people. So that's why they built Vlassopolis." He took out a tissue and wiped Barry's cheek. "Sorry, Barry. It's very hard not to spit when you say Vlassopolis. Oh dear, I've done it again."

"Really, it's no problem. . . ."

"Why couldn't they just have called it Vlassorina Towers?" said Jonty with a sigh.

"But who lives on all these other floors?" asked Barry.

"No one," said Jonty. "They sometimes give the apartments to some of their famous friends to stay in, when they're in town. You know. Finula Postalnarg. She's stayed here. Jatt Blatt. Monty from Monty and the Nose Hairs (obviously only Monty— none of the Nose Hairs). Imogen Le Bam-Bam, who, as I'm sure you know, designed the first-ever edible smartphone. Dickie Henderson-Bear, who dances on a carousel in—"

Ting! went the elevator, much to Barry's relief. He'd had just about enough of Jonty's name dropping, especially when the names were all people he hadn't heard of.

The elevator doors opened, not into a corridor as Barry expected, but straight into the penthouse flat. It was an enormous room, bigger than any Barry had ever seen, with windows on all sides, showing an amazing view of the city.

The room itself was really white: white walls, thick white rugs, paintings on the wall that seemed to be just blank white canvases, and on the very long white sofa, a white poodle, a white fluffy cat, and a long-haired white rabbit, looking at him curiously. Music was playing, piped in from all sides. Barry had just caught the lyrics—"He sleeps by the fire/

While we watch the news!"—when, from the ceiling, two white cages descended containing two figures, apparently asleep.

The cages reached the floor and their doors opened. The man looked up with a surprised face and sang: "And when one pops out!"

The woman looked up, danced into his arms, ballroom style, and leaned back, singing, "He looks confuuuuuused!!" Then they opened their mouths and pretended to bark. Eventually, the music stopped and, from their dance position, the man and the woman—clearly Vlad Mitt and Morrissina Padada or, if not, some lunatics who had broken in—said, together: "Barry—welcome to Vlassopolis!"

Jonty took out his tissue and wiped their combined spit off Barry's face.

CHAPTER FOUR

Barry had an amazing day with Vlassorina. Vlad showed him clips from his movies, and Morrissina showed him videos of all her hits. They took a photograph of him with the two of them putting their arms around him and posted it on something they called Birdynoise, and, because @Vlassorina had seventeen million "feeders," they got 20,000 people reseeding it to all their friends!

Morrissina wrote a song—well, she called a man

up who, twenty minutes later, sent her back a song—called "Barry, I Will Carry You," a really big, slow, emotional number like people do on *The* X *Factor* in the sing-off. "Barry/I will carry you/Whenever you fall/I'll be there standing tall . . ." it went, when she sang it for him.

It was a tiny bit awkward for Barry as she sort of sang it *at* him, with a backing track that the unnamed man who wrote it had sent via computer, and so Barry had to keep smiling for about five minutes. And then he realized that he probably shouldn't be smiling, that maybe he should look as if he was about to cry, like the judges always did on *The* X *Factor* when people sang these songs.

But, by the time he thought this, it was too late; she was hugging him, and Vlad, who (it turned out) had been filming it, was saying, "That'll be great. I'll get Jonty to put it up on MeMeMeTube."

Then, later, Vlad called—or possibly got Jonty to

call, Barry wasn't sure—Jamie Gherkiner, who was the most famous chef in this world, and he came around and prepared the most incredible snack for tea. Jamie said: "OK, Barry, mate! Whatcha fancy, me old darlin'?" And after Vlad had explained what that meant, it became clear that Barry could say literally the first thing that came into his head and Jamie would be able to make it, in Vlassorina's enormous stainless-steel kitchen.

"Er . . . sausage-flavored jelly?"

"No worries!"

"Doughnuts filled with cookie-dough ice cream . . . ?"

"Coming right up!"

"A whole roast chicken made entirely out of skin!"

"If you say so . . ."

"Salty bananas!"

"That's the side dish sorted."

"Sherbet pie!"

"My signature dish!"

Thirty minutes later, all this food was miraculously sitting on the huge white dining table, looking amazing. Barry couldn't believe it. There was a weird moment when he wasn't allowed to eat it straight away, but had to stand smiling by the table with Jamie and Vlad and Morrissina while Jonty took photos of them all—for *Good-bye!* magazine, he heard Morrissina say—although not as weird, to be honest, as the actual taste of salty bananas. Jamie looked a bit upset when Barry spat them out, but then he smiled again when Barry tucked into the sherbet pie. Everyone laughed and clapped at the huge cloud of white that exploded out of it when he dug his fork in.

"It matches the furnishings!" said Morrissina, and everybody laughed again, even Barry, who had no idea what she meant.

Then, after tea, which, apart from the salty

bananas, was absolutely delicious, Vlad said: "Right! Time to get ready!"

"Ready for what?" said Barry.

"Your party, of course!"

"Oh!" said Barry. "Right!"

"So we got a message from the Parent Agency that it's a . . ." He got out his phone, which, like the steering wheel of his car, was covered in diamonds and, Vlad had told him earlier, was a special gift from the people at Peach. ". . . hold on . . . James Pond party?"

"Bond."

Vlad looked up. "Definitely says Pond here. And the diamond aCommunicator—only one in the world—never lies."

"Um . . ."

"So who is this James Pond guy?"

"Well. He's like a secret agent who drives fast cars and fights evil and stuff."

"What?! Morrissina! Are you thinking what I'm thinking?!"

"I think I am, darling!!"

"I know you are."

"I know you are too."

"*Mmmmmmmmmm-mmmmm*," said their mouths as they kissed. *Urrrgggh*, thought Barry, waiting for them to finish.

"You're in luck, B-Man!" said Vlad when they finally stopped kissing.

"Er . . . why?" said Barry.

"Because this character James Pond sounds exactly like Dirk Large!"

"And," said Morrissina, hugging Barry again, "it's the premiere of the new Dirk Large movie tonight! With a big party afterward! At which *you* can be the guest of honor, Barry!!"

"Great!!" said Barry. "Um . . . just one thing. Er . . . Who's Dirk Large?"

Morrissina moved away from him, incredulous. Vlad also looked like someone had slapped him with a wet fish (as Barry's grandpa used to say, about surprised faces).

"You really don't know?" said Vlad. "Where have you been for the last ten years, my friend?"

"Er . . . somewhere else . . . ," said Barry.

Vlad stood up. He turned his head away from Barry and stared hard into the distance.

"Secret agent. Driver of fast cars. Battler of evil," he said. He turned back to Barry and mimed aiming a gun at him. "I . . . am Dirk Large. Of *Death in the Car.*"

"Except in number three, when they got Jackie Noodle to be him . . ."

"Yes, thank you, Jonty. Can you go and get my suit ready, please?"

CHAPTER FIVE

So that was why Barry was here now, on the red carpet, with loads of screaming fans and cameras everywhere flashing at him. He thought of how the three of them must look. He was wearing a tuxedo again, but not like the one he had worn at Bottomley Hall: this one was white and his bow tie was white with sparkly silver skulls on it. Vlad's tuxedo was also white; although he wasn't wearing his bow tie, he had it undone around his neck.

Morrissina was wearing a long white dress (not the same long white dress she'd been wearing earlier: this one showed quite a lot of her bosoms, for some reason).

Barry thought about that photograph going all around the world (well—*this* world), with him in the middle of it. It felt strange. But also very exciting.

When that picture was done, Jonty said to the cameras, "No more photos, guys, that's it!" and the three of them began to move away. Barry could hear the cries of his name from the photographers growing fainter.

Then, just before they passed through the doors of the cinema, he heard two more shouts of "Barry!" that sounded familiar.

He looked around. The cameras flashed again. He squinted and shielded his eyes. Looking into the crowd of photographers, he thought he saw, above one lens and below another, two faces. A man and a woman: the *same* man and woman he had seen in the Head's office, and briefly at Bottomley Hall. Looking at him with concern. And hope. Everyone there was looking at him with hope, of course, hope that he would turn to them and smile for the camera. But these two were looking at him with something else as well. Something he couldn't quite name.

"Where are you, my darling?" he heard Morrissina say.

"Come on, Barry," said Jonty into Barry's ear. "Vlassorina aren't used to being kept waiting. . . ."

"Sorry!" Barry said. Just before he entered the foyer, he turned once more to the throng of cameras, but couldn't see the two faces anymore.

The film was brilliant. Dirk Large was very like James Bond. He didn't drive an Aston Martin, didn't work for MI6, didn't have the code name 007, no secret gadgets, no people around him called letters like Q and M, and there were quite a lot of other differences, but he did kill a lot of people and sometimes, after killing them, he would say clever little jokes about how they died.

One time Dirk was in the Death Car, which was some kind of amazing Jeep/Formula One/Batmobile combo, and another car was trying to force the

Death Car off a cliff, but Dirk was a better driver and so the guy who was trying to kill him ended up going off the cliff instead. As he went over, Dirk said, under his breath: "Well, I guess *he's* reached the end of the road. . . ."

Which was *exactly* like something James Bond would've said.

Then, afterward, they went to an enormous party called, for some reason, an *after*-party. Barry didn't really understand that as he thought it meant there must have been another party before, but Jonty, who drove him there, explained that it meant the party *after* the film.

Barry had been expecting to drive to the party with Vlad and Morrissina, but he'd noticed that, when the cameras weren't on them, or when Jonty wasn't filming it to go on MeMeMeTube, Vlassorina seemed not to want to be with him quite as much. They were still really nice and smiley, but—as had happened with the car to the party—they'd wave and Vlad would say, "OK, Jonty, you take the B-Man!" and go off. It made Barry feel kind of weird, but he put it out of his mind because everything else was so exciting.

When they got to the party, which was in a huge hotel called the Hotel V that had a big V on top just like Vlassopolis, Jonty made sure Barry met up again with Vlad and Morrissina before they went in. Which meant that he had loads more photos taken, because there were loads more photographers waiting outside there too. It was starting to make his eyes hurt, looking into so many bright camera flashes.

Inside, they were led to a room. In the room were lots of other famous people. Barry was introduced to Finula Postalnarg, and Jatt Blatt, and Imogen Le Bam-Bam—who was chomping through her latest mobile phone, which was funny, although she didn't seem to think so when Barry laughed. But, although they all clapped and smiled and hugged Vlad and Morrissina when he was introduced as their son, Barry wasn't sure whether or not they were actually interested in him at all. He did get to meet Monty, who was quite friendly, but it got a bit awkward when Barry asked where the Nose Hairs were, since they hadn't been invited.

As Monty went off, looking embarrassed, Barry noticed Jonty standing there.

"Jonty?" said Barry. "Um . . . is this it? The whole party?"

"No," said Jonty. "Of course not. This is the VIP room."

"What does that mean?"

"It's a special room that they have at premieres and showbiz events where the really famous people can go and only have to talk to other really famous people."

"Oh."

Jonty nodded toward some doors. "The *real* party's happening out there."

"It is . . . ?"

"Yes," Jonty said. He checked his watch. "Shall we go and have a look . . . ?" He led Barry over to the doors. As they got nearer, Barry could hear the thump of music. Jonty opened the doors and the music suddenly got much louder. He and Jonty went through onto a balcony—an indoor balcony!—which looked out on the biggest room, hosting the biggest party that Barry had ever seen.

Another phrase that his grandpa used to say came into his head.

Oh my giddy aunt, thought Barry.

CHAPTER SIX

Hundreds of other people were in the bigger party room, dancing, talking, drinking, and moving about. There were six-meter-high screens all around the room, playing scenes from the movie, and in the middle of it stood an enormous replica of the Death Car. Loads of guests were walking up a huge staircase that led to the driver's door. Others were standing in groups on the seats. Some were climbing up and down on the spokes of the massive steering wheel.

The music that Barry could hear was pumping out from the giant stereo on the mammoth dashboard. (As Barry looked over the whole scene, he realized his mind was running out of ways of saying "big.")

All around the colossal

(phew—he'd thought of one more) car, there were enormous (and another!) guns, in the shape of Dirk Large's gun. But they weren't ordinary guns. As Barry watched, he saw Jamie Gherkiner going over to each one and heaving back the trigger; then out shot a huge (he'd given up—from now on, he was just going to use one word for big, and huge was it) chocolate arc into the air, around the car, creating above it a huge liquid net of chocolate.

"What do you think, Barry?" said Vlad, joining him on the balcony.

"It's amazing. . . ."

"It's going to get more amazing . . . ," said Morrissina, wafting through from the VIP room. Barry felt a breeze start up through his hair, which was strange as they were definitely indoors. Then he heard Jonty shout:

"OK, Sir and Madam V and, of course, Barry. Would you care to step this way." Barry looked over. Jonty had reappeared, but not on the indoor balcony— *hovering beyond the edge of the balcony*—in the pilot's seat of a helicopter! The door of the chopper was open and a small platform came out from it. Slowly, it connected to a gate in the balcony. A gate which Vlad and Morrissina were already walking through and on to the helicopter!

Barry rushed over and walked onto the platform. Morrissina held out her hand to steady him as he got into the helicopter.

"Where are we going? We only just got here . . . ," said Barry.

"We're not going anywhere, Barry," said Jonty as he buckled a seat belt across him.

"No," said Vlad. "We're just making an entrance!"

Then, following a signal from Jonty, the music changed to the theme music from the movie (which was more DA! DA! DA! than Dah Da-Da-Da/Dadada/Dah!da-da-da/Da-Da-Da/DAH-DAH!/Dadada) and the blades of the helicopter started whirring much faster.

Up they went, to the ceiling of the huge room, high above the crowd, who looked up as one. Morrissina and Vlad waved to them from inside the cockpit. Barry, not knowing what else to do, waved too. The crowd roared and clapped.

Jonty brought the helicopter down, expertly guiding it through the gaps in the chocolate net, weaving first one way then another. He hovered for a second over the roof of the Death Car, before bringing them down on top of a huge X painted in the middle of it. He turned a key and the blades stopped rotating.

"Right, Barry!" said Vlad. "Come and greet your public. . . ."

CHAPTER SEVEN

The three of them stepped out, still waving, into a bright spotlight. As the noise of the blades died down, the roar grew louder.

"Vlad?" said Barry, looking up. "Can I stand underneath that chocolate fountain with my mouth open? In fact, can I run from one chocolate gun-spray to another with my mouth open?"

"Yes, of course," said Vlad. Barry noticed that Vlad was suddenly holding a microphone. "But first of all—let's not forget: you're the guest of honor!"

"Ladies and gentlemen . . . ," he said, speaking into the microphone; his voice boomed out across the room. "Partygoers! *Death in the Car* 5 fans! Please put your hands together for tonight's guest of honor. We—and by we I mean me and Morrissina Padada, popularly known as Vlassorina, a brand name which we own and which is not to be used for commercial purposes by anyone else without written permission from our lawyers—proudly present our new son . . . Barry!!!"

There was another huge roar and another huge round of applause. Barry could see Vlad and Morrissina applauding too, by his side. Not knowing what else to do, he waved some more, even though his arm was really starting to hurt. This got another huge roar from the crowd, like he'd done something really amazing. He wished he had his scooter—which wasn't a great scooter, just a Razor without special stunt handlebars or anything—to hand, and then he could've done a flip or something. Something to *deserve* all that applause.

Underneath the noise of the clapping, Barry, still waving, whispered to Vlad: "Can I go and run around underneath the chocolate gun spray now?"

"Hmm?" said Vlad. "Yes, I guess so. But, first of all, a press conference!"

"Pardon?"

"Hey, Barry!" He looked around. About nineteen grown-ups had somehow appeared on the roof of the Death Car, with microphones and notepads and video cameras.

"Barry! Barry! Barry! Barry!"

Oh, *not again*, thought Barry.

"Barry! What's it like being Vlassorina's son . . . ?"

"Er . . . it's great . . ."

The ones with pads wrote that down. The ones with microphones nodded.

"Did you ever imagine in your wildest dreams that one day you'd be the son of the most famous couple in the world?"

"Um . . . no, I guess not . . ."

The ones with pads wrote that down. The ones with microphones nodded.

"Are you going to have your own range of perfumes, to go along with *Stink-Bombe*?"

"Er . . . yes, I suppose?"

"What's it going to smell of?"

"Um . . . poo and pee . . . ?" said Barry.

The ones with pads started writing that down, but then stopped and looked a bit upset. The ones with microphones glanced at each other nervously.

"Barry will be meeting a number of top designers," interjected Morrissina with a smile, "and we're all looking forward to smelling what they're going to create together."

"I will?" said Barry. She nodded. "Morrissina, can

I go and run around, catching the chocolate in my mouth, now?"

"Of course," she said. "Just one more tiny thing we need you for. And then you can do whatever you want!"

"Great!" said Barry, who by now was worried that the chocolate guns might be about to run out of ammo. "What is it?"

Vlad took out a piece of paper from the inner jacket pocket of his white tuxedo. But it wasn't just any old piece of paper. It was like a rolled-up scroll, the sort of thing you see on *Horrible Histories*. What was the word? *Parchment*. That was it. Vlad unrolled the parchment. There was some kind of writing on it. He held it out toward Barry with two hands.

"We *know*"—said Vlad—"I mean, why would you not? What's not to like? That you're already sold on us. We *know* you want to be our son. We also happen to know that you agree with us that the name Barry is . . . well . . . not quite right for the son of the most famous couple in the world."

"It isn't?"

"No," said Morrissina. "It really—well, it just doesn't work for us."

"Doesn't work?"

"No . . . ," said Vlad. "So what about changing it . . . ?"

Barry frowned. He didn't quite know what to say and, since it was a question he didn't immediately know the answer to, he dug his hands in his pockets. Where he felt his list.

Now he knew without getting it out that Number 2 on this list of things he blamed his parents for—really near the top—was "Calling me Barry." Another one of his grandpa's phrases (from before he lost his memory) popped into his head: *the bane of his life*. That's what his grandpa used to say about all sorts of things that really bothered him: the weather, the lines at the post office, the itchiness of his trousers. They were all the bane of his life. And, for Barry, the bane of his life was being called Barry. It always had been.

And yet suddenly he felt nervous about being called something else.

"Um . . . ," he said, "I guess that would depend on . . . what I was changing it to . . . ?"

"Exactly! So we were wondering about . . . ?" Vlad unrolled the parchment. In the middle was written, in huge letters, one word.

Barry looked at it for a while.

And a while longer.

Before saying:

"*Barrissina?*"

CHAPTER EIGHT

"**Y**es!" said Morrissina as Barry stared at her, dumbfounded. She clapped her hands together. "Barrissina! Doesn't it just sound divine!"

"I'm really glad you like it," said Vlad.

"You've got some lovely middle names as well," said Morrissina.

"They're in the small print," added Vlad.

Barry looked at the document. Squinting, he realized that the whole thing said:

I, *Barry Bennett, hereby renounce all claim to the name Barry Bennett, and any desire to ever again be called Barry Bennett, and accept fully the name* . . .

BARRISSINA ORANGE HAMLET BUNNY-CUTIE PIDDLYPIDDLYPIDDLY MITT.

"Orange?" said Barry.

"Like the fruit!" said Morrissina.

"Yes, I've heard of it," said Barry. "Bunny-Cutie?"

"So sweet!"

"Piddlypiddlypiddly?!"

"That was just something I threw in," said Vlad. "I'm crazy like that!"

"So . . . ," said Jonty, handing Barry a pen—it was covered in diamonds, like Vlad's aCommunicator and steering wheel, and felt heavy in his hand—"all you need to do is sign on the dotted line."

Vlad and Morrissina held the parchment up

between them. Vlad pointed. "Just there."

Barry heard a murmur in the crowd. It sounded like: "Sign it." And then, less like a murmur and more like a chant: "*Sign it. Sign it. Sign it.*"

"Er . . . look," said Barry. "It's true—although I have no idea how you found out—that I don't really like the name Barry. But now I think about it . . . I don't know that I *actually* want to get rid of it. It is my *name* after all."

"*Sign it. Sign it. Sign it,*" went the crowd, louder every time.

"And also, if I was going to get rid of it, I'd like a cool name. Like Lukas. Or Jake. Or . . ."

"Dirk?" said Vlad.

Barry thought about this. "No, not really."

"Sorry," said Vlad. He put his mouth to the microphone. "Are you saying that . . ." The crowd stopped chanting. ". . . Dirk *isn't* a cool name?"

There was a mass intake of breath. Barry could

feel hundreds of eyes upon him. "Er . . . no, it isn't . . ."

The crowd roared. But this time it wasn't a good roar. It was a bad roar. It was a bad roar completely covering up Barry's next words:

". . . not for me at any rate . . . I'm sure other people might think so . . ."

"Look, I've had enough of this," said Morrissina, not smiling for perhaps the first time since Barry had met her. "Sign the stinking form."

"Darling," said Vlad. "That's a swear."

"No it isn't."

"Well, technically it is," said Barry.

The crowd started up again, low and threatening: "*Sign it. Sign it. Sign it.*"

And this time, Vlassorina, together, joined in: "Sign it. Sign it. Sign it." They moved toward Barry, one "sign it" at a time.

"Sign it."

"Sign it."

"Sign it."

Eventually,

BARRISSINA

was right in front of Barry's eyes and "Sign it. Sign it. Sign it" was all he could hear in his ears. He shut his eyes and tried to stop his ears, but it was no good. He opened his eyes.

Down below, cameras flashed. Among the flashes, for a second, Barry thought he saw, lit up, the faces of the man and the woman who had been outside, looking at him with concern and hope and that something else he couldn't put his finger on. But it was a long way down and he couldn't quite make out their faces properly.

Barry turned back to the parchment.

"All right! I'll sign it!" he said.

The crowd roared—a huge roar and back to a good roar. Vlassorina looked at him with joy. They pushed the parchment closer toward him. He lifted the pen and wrote.

"Hip hip hooray!" said Vlad.

"Thank you, Barrissina!" said Morrissina.

"That's OK," said Barry. "Why don't you read it out loud?"

"I will," said Morrissina. "In fact, we'll do it together." They turned to face the crowd.

"I, Barry Bennett, hereby renounce all claim to the name . . . hang on, you've crossed a bit out here . . ."

"I'm very impressed that you managed to say that second part together," said Barry. "Carry on."

"I, Barry Bennett . . . hereby renounce all claim to the name . . . Barrissina. Orange Hamlet Bunny-Cutie Piddlypiddlypiddly Mitt."

Barry's prospective parents looked up, their faces stamped with confusion. Clearly, no one normally ever said no to Vlassorina. There was a gasp from the crowd. Imogen Le Bam-Bam actually fainted (although later doctors worked out that this was due to her having eaten a dodgy smartphone).

"And just a bit more, please," said Barry.

"And . . . ," they read, "I would like to be taken back to the Parent Agency."

"Signed Barry Bennett," said Barry Bennett, taking the parchment out of their hands.

WEDNESDAY

CHAPTER ONE

"**S**o . . . two parents down, as it were," said the Head. "Would you say either the Rader-Wellorffs or Vlassorina were, you know, on the short list?"

"Short list?" said Barry.

"To become your permanent parents . . . Are they in the frame? What would be the odds on either of them?"

Barry and The Secretary Entity were sitting in the Head's office again. The Head had already turned over the third 24-Hourglass, the green one. The four of them had watched the first grains trickle down in silence.

Barry didn't know much about odds, apart from when he and his dad were watching soccer together on TV and, at halftime, a man's enormous head would appear and say something like "Chelsea to win three to one . . . eleven to two on!" Barry didn't really understand what that meant, although his dad would sometimes bet some money based on what the man's enormous head was suggesting, and almost always lose it.

"I don't know," said Barry. "Not very good. The Rader-Wellorffs about five million to one. And Vlassorina about twice that much."

The Head looked shocked—both eyebrows went up this time, but not in a yes-I'm-so-clever-and-witty James Bond manner: just in a straightforward OMG! way.

"Write that down, Secretary One," said Secretary Two.

"I'm writing it dow—"

"No, don't," said the Head. Now it was The Secretary Entity's turn to look shocked. "Just . . . don't," he repeated. There was an awkward pause. TSE put their pads down.

The Head turned back to Barry. "So. Barry. You've still got three sets of parents left in your package. What kind would you like next?"

Barry took his list out of his pocket. It was looking torn and bedraggled now, and so creased it was becoming hard to read. But it was still clear enough (and anyway he knew it by heart) to read Number 3: "Being tired all the time."

"Fit," he said. "I'd like some really fit and strong parents, please. I'd like parents who *never* get tired."

It didn't take long for the next set of parents to appear. In fact, almost as soon as The Secretary Entity had found a match for the words FIT and

NEVER TIRED on the computer, a man and a woman appeared at the door of the Head's office.

"Hello!" said the man.

"Hello!" said the woman.

They were both wearing bright blue, all-over Lycra bodysuits, white headbands, and very big sneakers. "I'm Derek *Fwahm!* And this is my wife, Emily *Fwahm!* We got here as quickly as we could!"

"Which, as you may have gathered," said the woman, "is really, really quickly!"

"Hoor-hoor! Hoor-hoor! Hoor-hoor!" they said together, which Barry thought, but wasn't entirely sure, was laughter.

"Fwahm?" said Barry.

"No," said the man. "*Fwahm!* With an exclamation mark! Not a question one!"

"So you have to shout it?" said Barry.

"No," said the woman. "It's more the way you say it! We prefer to say it with this action!" She said,

"*Fwahm!*" while moving her hand sharply away from her, palm down. "Sort of an action word! It might go in a comic strip with something moving away from you very fast! A car! A rocket!"

"*Fwahm!*" said Derek *Fwahm!*, doing the hand action.

"*Fwahm!*" said Emily *Fwahm!*, doing it too.

"OK, I've got it," said Barry, who was beginning to wonder whether he should just ask the Head to start looking through the options for parents number four.

CHAPTER TWO

But he didn't.

Derek and Emily had brought Barry some running gear, so that they could sprint all the way to their house. There wasn't anywhere to change as they were on the street outside the Parent Agency. So, to protect his modesty, the *Fwahms!* ran around him very, very fast, forming a circle of speed which, from a distance, looked like a wobbly blue fence.

Back in his own world, at school, Barry had

sometimes gone running, and he'd worn a pair of white shorts and a Barcelona top from 2009 that was too small for him, but the *Fwahms!* gave him a child's version of their blue Lycra suits, a white headband, and sneakers. He thought it probably looked really embarrassing—the Lycra was very tight—but once he'd put it on he did feel like he could go faster than normal.

Then, once they started running, he was *sure* he was actually going faster than normal. The sneakers were really bouncy and the suit felt like it just glided through the air. The only problem was, however fast he went—and Barry was a pretty fast runner: he'd come second in the school cross-country run (and would've come first if Taj hadn't cheated by getting a secret ride halfway from his mom and dad)—he couldn't go nearly as fast as the *Fwahms!* Most of the time, they were at least a hundred meters in front of him. Then they'd stop and say, "Come on, Barry!

Nearly there!" When he got close to them, though, they'd be off again: *Fwahm!*

Eventually, to save time, Derek *Fwahm!* lifted Barry up and ran with him on his shoulders all the way to their house, which Barry wasn't sure about as he knew it might look quite babyish— but really, because Derek moved so fast, it was kind of fun. It was like riding a blue, Lycra-suited, two-legged horse.

After a while, Derek skidded to a halt— Barry actually pulled on some imaginary reins and went "Whoa!"—and put him down. In front of them was a large white building with the words *Sweat Shop* on its front.

"Here we are!" said Emily.

"Sorry, where are we?" said Barry.

"Our house!" said Derek who, like Emily, didn't seem able to say anything that didn't end in an exclamation mark. He got his keys out and approached the doors of *Sweat Shop*.

"That's a gym, isn't it?" said Barry.

"It used to be!" said Emily, taking his hand and leading him into it. "But now it's our house!"

Barry went into the building. There was

a lobby area with a wide desk at one end. "Oh, so you converted an old gym into a house?" he said, remembering that in his world the same thing had happened to an old church just off the A41.

"Nope!" said Derek. "We live in it just as it was!"

"So . . . ," said Emily, who by now was standing behind the desk. "Would you like membership of our house?!"

"Hoor-hoor! Hoor-hoor! Hoor-hoor!" they said together.

As it turned out, though, it was fun living in a gym. Particularly a gym that no one else apart from the three of them was allowed into. Barry liked having free run of the exercise bikes and the treadmills and the endless number of enormous rubber balls. He liked being able to drink as many energy drinks as he wanted. (The ones here, which came free out of the machines, were called *PowerFizz* and *Energyade*, and were purple and green and *very* bubbly.) And he liked that there were loads of TVs hanging above the treadmills. Except none of them seemed to be working.

"Ah!" said Derek, when Barry pointed this out. "We don't have normal TVs in our gym! Too easy to just stand and watch them! No! Get on and you'll see!"

Barry stepped on a treadmill and started running. As he got his speed up, the TV came on. It was a show called *Pop-Newz*, just starting. It had a title sequence with lots of different people singing a theme tune which went:

"Pop-Newz! Pop-Newz! More interesting than shoes!"

"Now, Barry, slow down a bit . . . !"

Barry slowed down to a quick walk. As he did so, the TV slowed down too. The singers started moving in slow motion, and the sound of their voices went all low and weird and stretched out, like ghost voices in films. *"Pooooppp . . . Newwwzzzz . . . Pooooopppppp . . . Newwwwzzz . . . Mooooorrrreee ffffuuuunnnn ttttthhhhaannnn a baddddd bruisssse . . ."*

"Right, now speed up!" said Derek. "As fast as you can go!"

Barry moved his legs faster and the TV went back to normal. Then he went faster still and all the singers started moving as if they were speeded up, and their voices became high-pitched, like they'd sucked on helium.

"Pop-Newz!Pop-Newz!Moreexcitingthanan electricalfuse!!!" they sang.

"It's designed to make sure you run at exactly the right speed!" said Derek. "Brilliant, isn't it?!"

"Yes," said Barry, which was all he could say, since he was completely out of breath. He noticed that the first item on *Pop-Newz* was a piece about Vlassorina. They were being filmed smiling at home with their new child, Patarina. Barry slowed down.

"*Weeeeeveeee alllllwwaaayys waaaannnnttteeed a girrrrrlllll . . . ,*" Vlad was saying, while bouncing Patarina on his knee.

"Maybe I'll do a bit more of that later," said Barry, getting off the treadmill.

"OK!" said Derek, who was in the middle of doing some jumping jacks.

"So . . . !" said Emily, who came skipping into the room—not skipping as in doing a hoppy, jumpy walk, but skipping, properly, with a big yellow jump rope—"we've got it all sorted for your party!!"

"The soccer party?"

"Yes!"

Barry had felt that, partywise, it was perhaps time for a change, the James Bond idea not having gone so well in the previous parental tryouts. So he had suggested to the Head that a soccer party would be equally to his liking. The Head had said he thought that would be right up the *Fwahms!'* street.

"Great!" said Barry.

"There's a place where we can have a soccer party right up our street!" said Emily, still skipping.

"Right! Yes, that's what the Head said. Although I thought, when he said that it was right up your street, he meant . . . it was something you'd be good at doing."

"It is!" said Derek. "But it also happens to actually *be* right up our street! At the end of this street is Wobbly Stadium!"

"Wobbly Stadium?"

"Yes!"

"Does it . . . um . . . wobble?"

"Only when there's a *lot* of people in it . . . !" said Emily. "Anyway," she continued, dropping the jump rope, but joining in with Derek's jumping jacks, "there's a game on tonight, a big international . . . !"

"Oh! Right! Who between?"

Derek smiled, stopped doing jumping jacks, and leaped on to a treadmill. The TV immediately started up. It was a different show from *Pop-Newz*, although with quite a similar theme tune. "Sports-Newz! Sports-Newz! Including stuff about teams nicknamed The Blues!" it went.

"So . . . ," said a voice-over when the theme tune had finished, "all eyes tonight are on Wobbly Stadium where, of course, everyone is gearing up for the big game between the United Kid-Dom and Boysnia-Herzogeweeny."

The TV showed a film of a group of kids of about Barry's age playing in front of enormous crowds. One team was in white and one in yellow.

"Oh!" said Barry. "They have kids' soccer on the TV here?"

Derek and Emily looked at him, amazed. "Of course!" said Emily. "I mean there's grown-up soccer as well! But that's not on TV! It's only kids' soccer that everyone's *really* interested in!"

"The last time these teams played," the voice-over continued, "United Kid-Dom won three to zero, mainly due to a fabulous hat trick scored by this boy among boys . . ."

The film cut to a boy on the United Kid-Dom side, beating four defenders, flicking the ball up with the backs of his heels, then bumping it up overhead before kicking it into the goal. The crowd went wild.

Barry squinted at the boy as he punched the air and ran toward the camera. "He looks like a younger version of Lionel Messi . . ." he said.

"Lee-oh-nel Messi?!" said Derek, still running, but not at all out of breath. "No, that's *Lionel* Tidy! The best kid player in the country!"

"What's Lee-oh-nel Messi like?!" said Emily.

"Well, a bit like that," said Barry. "Only from a place called Argentina. And grown-up. Although actually about the same size."

"But, despite that result, the United Kid-Dom still needs a win tonight to qualify for the Planet Birth Cup!" said the commentator.

The TV switched back to the studio.

"So . . . ," said Barry, ". . . is that where we're going for my party? To watch the game?"

Derek got off the treadmill, stopping the TV. He winked at Emily, who winked back. Emily suddenly ran out of the room, with a particularly quick *fwahm!*

"Going to *watch* it?!" said Derek.

Emily came back, again with a *fwahm!* She was holding in front of her a United Kid-Dom soccer jersey. She turned it around. On the back was printed the word "Barry."

"You're *playing*!! !!!" said Derek and Emily together, with more exclamation marks than Barry had ever heard.

CHAPTER THREE

"**O**K," said Big Col, "what I want from you, Bazza . . . is for you to stay in the hole, lying deep, holding up the ball when you need to, but in a free role right at the tip of the diamond, and we'll stick with the zonal marking one–three–two–three–one formation.OK? Although obviously I'd want you to track back when we go man to man."

"Right . . . ," said Barry, nodding. He shouldn't really have been nodding as, although Barry knew a lot about soccer, he had no idea what Big Col was talking about.

Big Col was the manager of the United Kid-Dom team. He looked like a fatter and balder version of Jonty/Peevish. He wore a big blue Puffa jacket with the initials BC on it. They were in the home changing room at Wobbly Stadium, and Barry was doing up his boots. He was very, very excited.

There were two reasons why Barry was here.

First, there was a tradition in this world that one ordinary boy, whose birthday it was (Barry had kept quiet about the fact that it wasn't *actually* his birthday for another three days), was allowed to play in every one of the United Kid-Dom's games.

Second, Derek and Emily *Fwahm!* turned out to be the team's fitness trainers. This reason was particularly important as it meant that they managed to sneak Barry in right at the top of the long list of kids who wanted to play. Barry had to admit that he was warming to Derek and Emily, having originally thought they were probably idiots.

"OK, Bazza's been given his instructions. The rest of you—say hello to Bazza!"

The team were all changing into their uniforms. They stopped and looked over at Barry. They didn't look that pleased to see him. They also looked very familiar.

"Jezza, Tezza, Mezza, Hezza, Quezza, Smezza, Sea Anemonezza, and Dave: I said say hello to Bazza!"

They mumbled a kind of growling hello and went back to putting on shin pads and tying shoelaces.

"So . . . ," said Barry, "you lot are the best kid players in the country? Wow! That's amazing, what with you all being from the same famil—"

"Um . . . ," said Big Col, interrupting and looking slightly embarrassed, "well, never mind about that. Though here's someone who is *definitely* one of the best players in the country." He led Barry over to one other player, who had his back to him, stretching his calf. "In fact, he could be the best player in the world. Our star man—Lionel Tidy!"

Their star man turned around. He smiled. "Bazza! *Hola!*" he said.

"Um . . . *hola* . . . ," said Barry.

"*Que pasa?*"

"Um . . . OK . . . thanks," said Barry.

"*Muy bueno,*" said Lionel.

Barry nodded and Lionel turned back.

Big Col bent down and whispered: "We don't know why he speaks like that. Some kind of weird language. But he's so good we don't ask."

Big Col gave Barry a thumbs-up and went back into the center of the changing room. Barry put on his United Kid-Dom top. His heart was beating with pride. In fact, his heart was beating *on* a pride, as the badge, which was next to his heart, was three lion cubs.

Big Col clapped his hands. Barry looked up.

"Right, everyone!" said Big Col. "Time for the warm-up!"

The team came out on to the floodlit field. The stadium was already three-quarters full. There was a roar as the crowd saw Lionel Tidy. He acknowledged it with a little smile. Then he ran to the touchline with a ball, flicked it up onto his right foot, then his left, then his right, then spun around while the ball was in the air and kicked it in a perfect arc all the way across the field to where Barry was standing. Barry raised his leg, and trapped it dead underneath his left foot. There was a burst of applause.

This is going to be brilliant! thought Barry. Then he heard a noise.

Fwahm!

Fwahm!

He looked around. Derek and Emily were now

standing in the center circle, wearing United Kid-Dom versions of their Lycra suits. They said together in a singsong voice:

"OK! Everybody! Gather round!!"

"Oh no . . . ," he heard Jezza say.

"Not again . . . ," said Tezza.

"Must we . . . ?" said Smezza.

"I wish I hadn't eaten that cheese," said Dave.

But they all ran over anyway, led by Lionel Tidy. Barry joined them. They lined up in a semicircle in front of Derek and Emily.

"Right!" said Derek. "Stretches first! Follow us!" Barry mentally prepared to do a bit of leg lifting and carrying—he thought he might try that one he'd seen on TV when soccer players bend one of their knees up backward and grab the cleat from behind—but then Derek and Emily together leaped up in the air and landed on the ground . . . *doing the splits.*

Ouch, thought Barry. But Lionel Tidy copied them

with ease. Jezza, Tezza, Mezza, and all the rest of them just about managed to do it, but without the jump and with a lot of groaning.

"Come on, Barry!" said Emily. "It's your party so you should be leading the way!"

"Uh . . . OK . . ." Barry did a frankly awful little jump in the air. He landed with his legs only slightly apart, and was planning to say, "Sorry, Derek and Emily, don't think I can do it," when his front foot slipped on the grass, and . . . well . . . *fwahm!* Next thing he knew he was bang on the ground with his legs as far apart as they could go.

"OWWWWW!" he said.

CHAPTER FOUR

"**T**hat's brilliant, Barry! Fantastic!" said Derek. "Best splits I've seen in a long time!"

"OWWWWW!" said Barry.

"Are you all right, Barry?!" said Emily.

"OWWWWWW*www* . . . ," he said.

"Breathe, Barry . . . remember to breathe . . . !"

"I don't think he can, Derek!"

"What! Quick! The Grübenschnitzel Maneuver!!"

"Of course! Grübenschnitzel to the rescue!!"

Suddenly, Derek had lifted Barry up under the arms and turned him upside down.

"Hey! I *can* breathe! I just banged my . . ."

Derek slapped him on the back. Again. And again.

"Ow! Ow! Ow!" said Barry.

"That's right! Get those lungs working again!" said Derek. He turned him back the right way up.

"OK?!" said Emily.

"Fghm . . . ," said Barry. It was the only word he could manage.

"Good! Now, everyone! Back to the warm-up! Sprint to the goalposts!"

The other players all started off. Barry didn't: he was still trying to recover from both the splits and the Grübenschnitzel Maneuver.

"Come on, Barry, we'll help you catch up!" said Derek. He and Emily grabbed hold of Barry's arms and started running; Barry couldn't help but go with them. The *Fwahms!* were so fast, it felt like being on the fastest treadmill ever. Barry had to move his still-aching legs as fast as they would go to stop just being dragged along the Wobbly turf. They ran him all the way to the United Kid-Dom goal (which was a long way—it might be kids' soccer, but it was a full-size, grown-up field) and then back to the center circle.

They stopped there. Barry couldn't breathe. He thought that must be the end of the warm-up.

The rest of the team arrived.

"Right!" said Emily. "Push-ups!"

"First one to a hundred wins a bottle of *PowerFizz!*" said Derek.

The team did a hundred push-ups. (Lionel Tidy won the bottle of *PowerFizz*.) Barry thought his arms were going to die and have to be buried separately from the rest of his body. And that . . . that . . . *must* be the end of the warm-up.

But then the *Fwahms!* said, "Right! Squat thrusts!"

and after that they said, "Right! Sit-ups!" and then after that, "Right! Head-furtles!" which was a kind of rolling neck movement that Barry had never heard of, and after that, "Right! Back twists!" which was an exercise so painful you don't even want to know about it, and after that, "Right! Bottom splats!" which was just as painful and also quite embarrassing.

After all that, it *still* wasn't the end of the warm-up. But luckily Derek and Emily were distracted by the arrival on to the field of the Boysnia-Herzogeweeny team for *their* warm-up.

The Boysnia-Herzogeweeny team didn't come on very quickly. In fact, they strolled on. Their fitness coach was a very fat man—even fatter than Big Col—with a wide mustache, the tips of which went down to his chin. He was wearing a large furry coat and carrying a chair. He got to their penalty area, put the chair down, and sat on it. Next to the chair he placed a large music player.

"*Shmole. Farhstoonken,*" he said. " Vvvvvarrrm-up!!"
He pressed a button on the music player.

"*Varstaaaa! Varstaaa! Fadooodle dunka missha! Barstahti bumpa-bumpa pooh-ic-nushpie!*" sang a voice.

The words didn't mean much to Barry, but the tune was really like "My Dog's Surprised by His Own Farts." After a while, it became clear that this *was* in fact what it was: a Boysnia-Herzogeweenian version of the song—called "Mi Canan Dist Vot-Vos-Dat? Ven Hist Bloots!"—because the Boysnia-Herzogeweenian team, perfectly in time, started doing the dance. All of them curled up into little balls; then looked up with a surprised face; then got up on all fours and pretended to bark.

The trainer with the big mustache watched them for about two minutes, then switched off the music player. "Vvvvvarrrm-up finished. Vell done."

The Boysnia-Herzogeweenian team got up and started walking back toward the changing rooms.

The United Kid-Dom team had only stood and watched while they did their dance. Emily and Derek looked a bit surprised by the other team's warm-up, but, after they'd gone, clapped their hands and said:

"Right! One hundred big-toe bends! Then one hundred eyelash presses!"

But, even before they had time to demonstrate a big-toe bend, Big Col came on to the field and said: "Don't be stupid, Derek and Emily. The match is about to start!"

CHAPTER FIVE

The match kicked off after the national anthems. Barry didn't know the words to the United Kid-Dom one, but it had a very grand tune, and he could just about make out the lyrics that all his teammates (and the crowd) were singing:

We are the United Kid-Dom
Oh yes we are
Kids can choose their mom and dad

La la la la la la laaaa!

. . . which seemed a bit on the nose about this world, but at least it was simple enough to allow him to join in the third time around. The Boysnia-Herzogeweeny anthem seemed to be—if Barry's ears didn't deceive him—an orchestral version of "My Dog's Surprised by His Own Farts," but he assumed he must have got that wrong.

There was also an awkward incident before the anthems, when the teams lined up to have their hands shaken by the head of the United Kid-Dom Soccer Association, who turned out to be Lord Rader-Wellorff. (This, it suddenly struck Barry, *might* just have been the reason why Jeremy, Teremy, Meremy, and all the others had got into the national team . . . .)

When Lord Rader-Wellorff saw Barry in the line-up, he looked shocked, and for a moment it seemed as if he was going to refuse to shake Barry's hand—like Barry had seen soccer players do from time to time in his world. But then he said: "Oh well, let's let bygones be bygones—eh, Jeremy, Teremy, Meremy, et cetera, et cetera?"

"Da-ad! We're called Jezza, Tezza, Mezza, et cetera, et cetera here!"

"Oh. Sorry, Jezza, Tezza, Mezza, et cetera, et cetera."

And he shook Barry's hand.

Lionel Tidy kicked off and passed the ball to Jezza, who passed it back to Lionel, who ran forward. Barry tried running on the wing alongside him, but then he realized that he was exhausted. Derek and Emily's warm-up had completely tired him out.

OK, thought Barry, *I'll just hang back for the first few minutes, to give myself some time to recover.* So he stopped running and, for about six minutes, he just watched, hardly moving from the halfway line. The United Kid-Dom team seemed to be in control, with Lionel dominating most of the play around the Boysnia-Herzogeweeny area. But the Boysnia-Herzogeweenians were good defenders, and so far no one had managed to get a shot in on their goal. Then Barry heard a shout.

"Oy!"

He turned. Big Col was standing on the touchline.

"What are you doing, Bazza? Get up there!! We need you!"

"I will!" said Barry. "I'm just waiting till I recover from the warm-up!" He said this while staring at Derek and Emily *Fwahm!*, who were standing on either side of Big Col. The whole thing looked like some kind of ad for a weight-loss program.

"What do you mean?!" said Derek. "That was our special *easy* warm-up!"

"And, more importantly," shouted Big Col, "there's only one minute left to play!!"

"Pardon?" said Barry. He looked up at the big

electric clock hanging above the crowd behind the goal. "We've only been playing for six minutes."

"Yes!" said Big Col. He turned to Derek and Emily. "I thought you told me he'd played soccer before?"

"He did tell us that, Big Col!" said Emily.

"Well then, why doesn't he know that a soccer match is SEVEN MINUTES LONG?!"

Barry frowned. "Seven minutes? That's ridiculous!"

"Oh, and how long should it be, clever clogs?" said Big Col.

"Ninety minutes!"

Big Col and Derek and Emily looked at each other. "Hoor-hoor! Hoor-hoor! Hoor-hoor!" they all went, holding on to each other. "Ninety minutes!"

"I'd like to see anyone last ninety minutes after one of our warm-ups!" said Emily, wiping away a tear.

"Anyway," said Big Col, breaking out of it, "never mind about that nonsense. Now you've only got forty-five seconds left!"

"There might be injury time, chief!" said Derek.

"Only about two and a half seconds," said Big Col, shaking his head. "And we need a goal! So get down there!"

Barry looked over. Lionel Tidy had the ball by the corner flag, hemmed in by three defenders. The referee was checking his watch. There was no time to argue about the stupidness of matches being seven minutes long. He started running.

It really was a long way from the center line to the penalty area on a proper soccer field. Barry had never thought about it before. Sometimes, when he was watching soccer on TV with his dad, and Chelsea (the team they supported) was playing, his dad would shout at a player for not chasing after the ball fast enough, and Barry would join in, shouting, "Slowpoke!" or "Come on, what's the matter with you?" But, as his heart started to pump faster and his legs began to ache, Barry Bennett thought that he would never shout things like that ever again. In fact, he thought he might shout, "Well done for getting there at all!" whatever speed they were running at.

Lionel Tidy still seemed a long way away and the clock was ticking down. Eventually, Barry was within shouting range of the United Kid-Dom's great star.

"Lionel!!" he shouted. He wasn't sure Lionel could hear as Barry was on the penalty spot and Lionel had only come in a little way from the touchline, still closely marked. Also, Barry was so tired by now, his voice came out as a tiny breathless squeak. But Lionel looked up. Barry shouted again.

"On my head!" he said. "Cross it!"

Squeak squeak squeak was how his own voice sounded to Barry. Too quiet—there was no chance Lionel could make out what he was saying. He glanced up. The clock said 6:43. Which meant there were seventeen seconds left.

"Tidy! CAN YOU NOT KICK IT?!" shouted Barry as loud as he could. He jumped up and down to try and make his intentions clearer, and also to make himself seen above the heads of the Boysnia-Herzogeweenian defenders. Which made him even more tired. He didn't know when he'd ever felt so tired.

Lionel looked over and then, as if someone had pushed a button somewhere on his body, sprang into action. He whirled around, like a spinning top, creating what seemed like a little hurricane at his feet, which the ball got caught up in. It rose in the air and then Lionel threw himself horizontally at it, like he was lying on a magic carpet, with one foot out. That foot connected beautifully with the ball—*bang!*—and it sailed off the wing toward the penalty area.

Barry was still jumping up and down. He watched

as the ball curved through the air. Through a mist of exhaustion, he could hear voices.

"Bazza! Bazza! THAT'S ALL YOURS!! EVERY TIME!!" That was Big Col.

"Breathe, Barry, breathe!!" That was Emily *Fwahm!*

"Remember to bend your legs as you land!!" That was Derek *Fwahm!*

"Barry!" He wasn't sure who that was. It was a female voice: someone in the crowd. But he'd heard it somewhere before.

"You can do it, Barry!" He wasn't sure who that was either. A male voice nearby. That he'd also heard before.

The ball was a few meters away now. He had to leap high, like a salmon, to get over the big Boysnia-Herzogeweenian defenders. He didn't want to look away, but for a second he did; and there they were in the crowd *again*: the mysterious man and woman, looking at him, with concern and hope. And the something else that Barry couldn't quite name.

He didn't have time to think about what that might be, though, because he needed to turn his head back toward the ball.

He swung his neck as it came flying in from his right-hand side and *fwahm!* It flew off his forehead exactly as it was supposed to, toward the goal, toward what his dad called the postage stamp . . . .

He saw the Boysnia-Herzogeweenian keeper jump toward it. He saw him stretch his fingers. But then Barry starting falling down again, having reached the highest point of his jump.

And, as he fell, he looked up, trying to see the ball, but all he could see was that Wobbly Stadium was indeed wobbling.

That *everything* was wobbling: the goals, the crowd, the defenders, the referee, even the enormous digital clock. Even the roar of the crowd as the ball went in, or was saved—he couldn't tell—sounded all wobbly. Perhaps it was one of those times when, like Emily *Fwahm!* had said, there were too many people in the stadium, he thought, just before he fell on the ground, fast asleep.

THURSDAY

CHAPTER ONE

"**W**ell," said the Head, "it was a great goal."

"Was it?" said Barry.

"Yes. I watched it on *Game of the Night*. Just a shame that afterward you had to be carried off."

"I *was* very, very tired."

"You must have been. I think it's the first time a player's ever been on a stretcher with a pillow, a blanket, and a teddy."

"Who gave me the teddy?"

"Emily *Fwahm!*"

"That was nice of her. . . ."

"Yes. Are you interested then, in them being your parents . . . ?"

"No," said Barry firmly. "Too tiring."

The Secretary Entity exchanged a glance and wrote down a word.

Barry looked over at their pads. He could see an F . . . a U . . . an S . . . another S . . . and what looked like the beginnings of a Y.

Then the Head said: "Well! Two more days left of your package. At least you've had a good night's sleep before this one." He turned over the fourth 24-Hourglass, the blue one. He looked at it: his eyebrow went up and then down again. More like a twitch than a raise. "You really need to—you know—get on with this, Barry. I'd really rather not leave it all till the last minute."

"Well, I have to do the whole package," Barry said.

"No you don't," said the Head. "If you find some parents you like, we can stop there and then not have to worry about . . ."

There it was. The trailing off.

"Worry about what?" said Barry.

The Head looked to The Secretary Entity despairingly.

". . . about which one to choose!" said Secretary One.

"Yes!" said Secretary Two.

"Exactly!" said the Head. "Write that down, Secretaries."

There was a short pause. "Really?" said Secretary Two.

The Head coughed nervously. "Anyway, Barry. What kind of mom and dad would you like to try out next?"

Barry took out his piece of paper. He'd covered a lot of the ground on the list already. He'd had parents that weren't boring; that were famous; that weren't poor; that weren't tired all the time.

But then he saw Number 6: "Being REALLY, REALLY, REALLY strict."

He couldn't believe it had taken him so long to say it.

"I'd like parents who let me do whatever I want, please!"

What happened after Barry said this wasn't quite the same as usual. The Head found some parents quickly, but they didn't appear quickly. In fact, they didn't come and pick Barry up at all, they just sent a message saying that he could arrive at their house "whenever he kind of, like, wanted?"

So the Head got PCs 890 and 891 to take Barry to where they lived.

They took a bus out of the city into the countryside. After a while, they passed a large sign with an arrow on it which said THE SEA. Barry sat on the backseat, in between Taj and Lukas, or PCs 890 and 891, as he was now properly starting to think of them.

"How's it going? Have you found the right parents yet?" said PC 890.

"I don't think so . . . ," said Barry.

"Hmm," said PC 891. "How old are you again?"

"I'm ten in two days."

Both of them looked at him sharply.

"Two *days*?" they said together. They looked worried. To be honest, they *sounded* worried too.

"Yes," said Barry. "Actually, about that. The Head said something . . . *happens* to children if they don't find the right parents by the age of ten. But he didn't say *what*." The PCs carried on staring at him; now they were looking not just worried, but uncomfortable. "Do you know?"

"Well . . . ," said 890, "I've heard—I mean, I don't *know* obviously 'cause I found my mom and dad when

I was like . . . seven! But I've *heard* . . . ," and here he looked around surreptitiously *and* he lowered his voice, almost to a whisper, "that you go into this really . . . really . . . dark—"

"So! Anyway!" said 891, interrupting loudly. "I gather you had a day with the Rader-Wellorffs! Is that true?"

"Well, yes . . . ," said Barry. "But, 890, can you just carry on with what you were going to tell me— about what happens when—"

"They'd be *amazing* parents! So much money!" said 890.

"Uh . . . they do have a lot of money . . . but . . ."

"And then the word at the Agency was that you got a shot at V*lassorina!*" said 891.

"Wow! Really? Did you?" said 890.

"Yes," said Barry. "But listen . . ."

"And they didn't do it for you either?"

Barry sighed; they were clearly not going to answer

his questions about the . . . thing . . . that happened to unparented ten-year-olds. He shook his head.

"OK . . . ," said 890, looking out of the window.

"Yeah. OK . . . ," said 891, looking out of the other window.

"Hey," said Barry, suddenly feeling angry. "The Rader-Wellorffs were crazy! They wanted me to shoot a bird! And Vlassorina, they wanted me to change my name to Barrissina! And the *Fwahms!*—"

PCs 890 and 891 both turned around at once.

"You had the *Fwahms!* as well?!" said 890.

"Blimey! Did they get you a game for the United Kid-Dom?" said 891.

"Oh, they did!" said 890. "That was *you*! I saw you on TV being carried off hugging a teddy. . . ."

"Well, yes. They did. That was me," said Barry.

They stared at him.

"You got to play at Wobbly Stadium!" said 890. "For the national team!"

"And you *still* . . . ," said 891, ". . . didn't think you'd found the right parents?"

Barry opened his mouth. But then he didn't know what to say. He looked down, a little ashamed, and thought to himself: OK. *I'm really going to try and like these next ones.*

CHAPTER TWO

The bus dropped them off by a large field, on a cliff. In the middle of the field, which had a lot of cows and sheep in it, stood a very colorful tent: mainly green, but also red and orange and blue and spray-painted with words like LOVE and PEACE and, strangely, NEIL.

Next to the tent was an old double-decker bus, exactly like the ones from Barry's world (well, exactly like the ones that *used* to be in Barry's world in the old days and that he still sometimes saw on TV in old films set in London). The PCs weren't all that keen on trudging across the muddy field to get to the tent and not sure what to do when they got there.

"Do we knock?" said PC 890.

"Knock on what?" said PC 891.

PC 890 looked at the tent doubtfully. There was a zipper holding the canvas together. "The . . . door . . ."

PC 891 shrugged, made a fist, and had a go. But his hand just folded into the canvas with a tiny shushing sound.

"Hmm. What do you suggest?" said 891, withdrawing his hand.

"We could call them," said 890.

"Call them what?"

"No, I mean . . . Mr. Cool?! Mrs. Cool?!" PC 890 shouted. "Are you in there?"

There was a shuffling inside the tent. Then a man's

voice said: "Do you, like, have a search warrant?"

PCs 891 and 890 looked at each other and at Barry, confused.

"Um . . . no . . . We're from the Parent Agency. . . ."

"Oh! Yeah! Cool!"

The zipper came down, sticking a couple of times as it went. Out of the tent came a thin man with a large shock of curly brown hair and an equally curly big beard, wearing pajamas.

"Sorry to wake you, sir," said PC 890. He checked his watch as he said this: it was half past two in the afternoon.

"Hey, no worries, man. So which one of you is, like, Barry?"

"Er . . . me . . . ," said Barry, putting his hand up.

"Cool," said the man. "I'm Elliott."

As he said this, a woman pulled the zipper farther down and came out of the tent. She was quite a large lady in a flowery dress. "Hi. I'm Mama Cool," she said. Then she looked at PCs 890 and 891 and said: "Do you work for The Boy?"

She had an accent a little like Barry had heard back in his own world, on a holiday his family once went on, to Cornwall. They had stayed at a bed-and-breakfast in a place called Coverack where the owner, also quite a large lady, was very proud of how strong her tea was. "You could stand your spoon up in this, my loves!" she would say as she put down the cups for Barry's mom and dad, every breakfast.

"I'm sorry?" said PC 890.

"Well," said PC 891, "we work for *a* boy."

"Hmm, I'd normally give you a much harder time," she said. "But I won't today because you've brought us…our son!!!"

She opened her arms and gave Barry a hug. She smelled of mud and horse poo. But in sort of a nice way.

"OK, PCs," she said, still holding him, "be off

with you. Because, once we start parenting Barry, we don't want you and your rule books around no more!!"

"OK," said PC 890.

"OK," said PC 891. "Take care!"

And they left, waving politely.

CHAPTER THREE

Barry and Elliott and Mama Cool went inside the tent, where it was much nicer than Barry was expecting. There were lots of candles in glass lamps and loads of cushions, and a really wide bed made out of furry blankets, and a big shaggy dog who jumped up and licked Barry's face as soon as he came in.

"This is, like, Neil," said Elliott.

"Oh!" said Barry. "That's why it says Neil on the outside of the tent."

"No, that's the name of the shop we got it from. *Neil's Tents.*"

"Oh," said Barry.

"So, Barry," said Elliott. "Welcome, man. To our, like, world?"

"Yes!" said Mama Cool. "And, in our world, anything you want to say or do: just say it or do it!"

"Yeah, that's how we, like, roll?"

"OK . . . ," said Barry. There was a short pause when no one quite seemed to know how to react to this statement. Barry smiled awkwardly at his potential parents; they smiled back. Then he said: "Butt."

Elliott Cool frowned. "Sorry?"

"Butt." Barry said it a bit louder the second time.

"Like, where?"

"No. You said I could say anything . . . so . . . BUTT!!!"

"Oh, I get it!" said Mama Cool. "Yes! Butt!!"

"Right . . . right . . . ," said Elliott. "Butt, yeah. Poo. Like, smell? Cool . . ."

"Butt!" said Barry, again. "Butt butt butt butt butt butt! Poo pee fart butt willie poo butt. Vomit and booger and diarrhea!"

Elliott and Mama Cool clapped and laughed.

"Awesome, Barry . . . ," said Elliott Cool. "What about, like, turd?"

"Or stinking?" said Mama Cool.

"Really?" said Barry. "I can say stinking?"

Elliott Cool smiled at his wife. She smiled back.

"As we said, Barry," said Mama Cool, "you can say or do *whatever* you like . . . ."

Barry took a deep breath. "Stinking turd!" he said.

Elliott and Mama Cool laughed and clapped again. Barry laughed and clapped too, even though the idea of a stinking turd made him feel a bit sick.

"Would you like something to eat, my love?" said Mama Cool after Barry had finally run out of all the nasty words he knew.

"Yes, please," he said. The swearing had become quite tiring by the end and he needed something to get his energy back.

They went outside again and around the back of the tent where a fire was burning, with an enormous stainless-steel pot on it. Mama Cool took the top off the pot and looked in.

"Mmmm. Mung Bean Muck-Muck . . . ," she said. She produced a wooden bowl and a ladle and dug into the pan. Two seconds later, Barry was staring at a meal of what looked like grimy yellow porridge.

Elliott and Mama Cool sat cross-legged on the floor with their bowls of Mung Bean Muck-Muck. They tucked in.

"Hmm, Mama," said Elliott, "this is, like, the best Muck-Muck ever?"

"Thanking you, husband-o'-mine. Hey, Barry, you're not eating . . . ."

"Yes . . . I . . ." Barry dug his spoon in. He raised the Muck-Muck to his lips. He put it in his mouth. It tasted like a melted brick.

He felt he should do his best to eat it. Otherwise, he thought, he'd seem rude. But then Barry remembered something about these parents. About what they'd just said.

"I don't want it," he said.

Elliott and Mama Cool looked up from their bowls.

"Sorry, Barry, man, couldn't quite understand you," said Elliott. "It sounded like you said *mmmi mdon mwan bbbliiit*?"

Barry chewed as best he could, for about ten seconds, then shut his eyes and, forcing his throat open, gulped down the spoonful of Muck-Muck. Mouth now clear, he said: "I don't want the Mung Bean Muck-Muck. It's disgusting. Can I have sweets instead, please?"

Elliott's spoon stopped halfway toward his mouth, and Mama Cool looked a tiny bit hurt, but, after a moment's pause, Elliott said: "Yeah, man, whatever. Let's get in the, like, bus?"

CHAPTER FOUR

They drove to the nearest village in the double-decker bus. Barry sat up on the top deck, near the front, enjoying the view. The village itself looked familiar. And it was. A big sign on the main road in said *Bottomley Bottom*. But, before they got to the gates for Bottomley Hall, the bus turned off toward a main street where there was a shop called *Bottom Sweets*.

It was an old-fashioned sweet shop, like the ones

in Barry's world which *pretended* to be old-fashioned sweet shops. A tinkling bell rang when he and Elliott and Mama Cool went in. Behind the counter were hundreds of high jars of old-looking sweets, pink and green and yellow, and frosted with sugary powders. It smelled of fruit; or at least of all the flavors of fruit that are impersonated by chemicals in sweets.

A man stood behind the counter in a white coat, with the tips of a series of pens visible in his top pocket. He looked a little like Peevish/Jonty/Big Col, only this time he was bald and wore glasses.

"Hello, like, Mr. Muddle?" said Elliott.

"Hello, Elliott! Hello, Mrs. Cool!" said Mr. Muddle, nodding at each of them in turn and smiling. "What can I do for you today?"

They gestured toward Barry, who was standing in between them.

"This young guy would like some, y'know . . .

sweets?" said Elliott.

"Oh!" said Mr. Muddle. "Well, that's what we specialize in here at *Bottom Sweets*!"

Continuing to smile, he lifted his arm. A little stiffly, he swung it behind him, in what Barry realized was a grand gesture, toward *Bottom Sweets*'s collection of jars.

"What would you like, young sir?" he said. "Sherbet Bing-Bongs? Pear Mists? Strawberry Slivers? Choccy Nits? Salt Henrys? Bitey Quarters? Nutty Drops? Fizzy Pearls? Sugar Sugars?"

"Er . . . do you have any sour sweets?" said Barry.

Mr. Muddle's face broke into an even bigger smile. "Aha! A connoisseur of the taste contradiction, are we? A delighter in the mouth dichotomy? A savorer of flavor danger?"

"Pardon?"

"You like sour sweets."

"Yes."

"Right. Well, we stock all the usual—Toxic Death, Sour Bads, Mouth Pursers, et cetera, et cetera But . . ."—he produced from his pocket a large gold key—". . . I suspect that with a sourerer of your level, we need to go . . . *sourer*. Eh? We need to turn the sour dial up . . . to thirteen!"

"Yes, please!" said Barry.

Mr. Muddle smiled even wider and bent down under the counter.

They could hear the sound of a key going into a lock. It was very clanky. Then what sounded like a rusty metal door being opened slowly and creakily. As if Mr. Muddle was opening the door to a haunted house rather than a sweet container.

"Er . . . ," said Mama Cool. "These sweets . . . will they be . . . ?"

"Yes?" said Barry.

"Nothing," she said. "Do what you want!"

Mr. Muddle's face appeared above the counter

again, his grin now looking quite crazy. He held in his hand a plastic tube. The tube was covered in skulls and radioactive signs. He turned it around, to display what it was called, at the same time saying the name out loud:

"A-BOMBS!" he said in a deep, frightening voice. "Where the A stands for . . . Acid!!"

"Great!" said Barry, taking the tube.

"Beware!" said Mr. Muddle, still in the same voice. "Beware the sour sensation, beyond anything ever conceived before, more power—"

"These'll be fine!" said Barry. And he opened the tube and popped one into his mouth.

Now, in his world, Barry thought of himself as something of a sour-sweet champion. He prided himself, when Lukas and Taj were around, on eating even the sourest of sweets and not reacting; on looking, in fact, as if nothing at all was going on behind his lips.

For the first five seconds of the A-Bomb, it was all business as usual. Mr. Muddle and Elliott and Mama Cool looked on, clearly concerned. Mr. Muddle said: "Um . . . I was going to suggest you just took a little lick to begin with . . ." But Barry kept sucking on the sweet while doing a "no problem" shrug, like he did at home.

And then his mouth exploded.

CHAPTER FIVE

It was actually like someone had dropped a real atom bomb on Barry's tongue. Well, it wasn't *actually* like that as that would have meant that his mouth would have *actually* exploded, along with his head, and *Bottom Sweets*, and most of Bottomley Bottom; but it felt really, really bad. Like the sweet was made of lemon, sugar, AND THE CORE OF A SUPERNOVA.

Barry opened his mouth and silently screamed.

"Oh my God!" said Elliott Cool.

"Mouth emergency!" said Mr. Muddle. "Mouth emergency!"

"What should we do?!" said Mama Cool.

Barry continued to move his face from side to side with his mouth open and his eyes wide with horror, like a baby who's accidentally eaten a chili.

"OK," said Mr. Muddle. He looked him straight in the eyes. "Barry. Lie down."

Barry did as he was told. He lay down in the middle of *Bottom Sweets*. His mouth was still open.

"Mr. and Mrs. Cool? Could you form a line to the sweets behind the counter?"

Barry heard some shuffling. His mouth was still open.

"Right. I'm going to shout out the name of a particular cocktail of sweets that I think, mixed together in Barry's mouth, will counteract the effect of the A-Bomb. It's a long shot, but it might just work."

"Like, OK?" he heard Elliott say. "You pass me the jar, Mama C!"

"Right, my love!" said Mama Cool.

"Sugar Sugars!"

Barry heard the sound of something rattling overhead. He looked up. Mr. Muddle was standing over him with a jar of bright white cubes.

"Whatever you do, Barry," he said, "don't shut your mouth . . . ." He tipped the jar forward and poured into Barry's mouth two Sugar Sugars. Barry could just about taste the sweetness underneath the raging sourness.

"Don't eat them yet!" said Mr. Muddle.

"Orggghmff . . . ," said Barry.

"Good boy."

Then, one by one, Mr. Muddle called for all the other jars.

"Banana Balls!"

Two of them went in.

"Caramel Hi-Kools!"

Four of them.

"Nougat Naughties!"

One of them.

"Toffee Snakes!"

Half of one of them. Mr. Muddle broke it and ate the other half while dropping the first half into Barry's mouth like a piece of spaghetti.

"And finally back to basics: pass me the Sherbet Bing-Bongs!"

Three of them. Barry had never felt his mouth so full of sweets. He'd never felt his mouth so full of anything.

"OK, Barry, now sit up. . . ." Barry did as he was told. Elliott and Mama Cool were standing there, looking worried, holding a number of open jars.

"And . . . crunch!!!" said Mr. Muddle.

Barry finally managed to shut his mouth, bringing his teeth down on the amazing confectionary mix in there. And Mr. Muddle was right: the incredible blend of sweetness overwhelmed the sourness of the A-Bomb, bringing the feeling inside his mouth back to normal. He bit, he chewed, he swallowed.

"Hmm," he said, looking up at the relieved faces of Elliott and Mama Cool and Mr. Muddle. "Quite nice actually. Can I have another A-Bomb?"

CHAPTER SIX

On the bus back, Barry decided to sit in the front with Elliott and Mama Cool. Elliott was driving and Mama Cool was sitting next to him. Barry noticed that they were both looking a little white and tense.

"So anyway, Barry, your party . . . ," said Mama Cool.

"Oh yes! What kind of party should I have?"

"Yes, well, obviously you should do . . . um . . ."

Elliott put a hand on his wife's knee. "Um. You

sure you, like, want to say this?" he said quietly.

"No, Elliott. We're committed to this way of life and we shall continue to be so whatever . . . the cost . . ."

"Yeah. Course, Mama. You're, like, right . . . ?"

"Barry. As we said at the start, you should always do exactly what you feel like doing. So you should have whatever party you feel like having!!"

By now, the bus was approaching the field with the Cools' tent in it. Barry thought for a moment. "OK," he said.

"Right! That's all the cows on the bus! Let's start the engines!"

Elliott and Mama Cool looked on from about ten meters away. They were clutching each other's hands. Elliott was shaking his head. Mama Cool may have been crying. But she was still managing to hold on to a spotty tablecloth knotted on to a stick which Barry had decided would serve well as a checkered flag.

The James Bond and soccer parties not having worked that well with the other parents, Barry had decided to just work with whatever was in front of him: to go with the flow—which was something else he had heard Elliott and Mama Cool say.

So what he'd suggested for a party this time was: *Animal Car Wars*.

This is how you play Animal Car Wars. You fill up whatever vehicle happens to be at hand with whatever animal happens to be at hand. Then you fill up another vehicle with whatever other animal happens to be to hand. Then you race each other, and all forms of banging, knocking, and animal throwing are allowed.

It had taken a while to fill the bus, and had involved quite a lot of Elliott and Mama Cool falling over while pushing and shoving and getting covered in manure, but now all the cows were on. Some of them had their heads poking out of the windows, especially on the top deck. There had been a lot of aggrieved mooing. Plus a bit of aggrieved barking, which was confusing at first, until it became clear that Neil had got on the bus as well and was squashed underneath one particularly bloated udder.

The other car in the race was the Rolls-Royce limousine from Bottomley Hall. Barry had asked Elliott and Mama Cool to invite Jeremy, Teremy, Meremy, Heremy, Queremy, Smellemy, Sea Anemone, and Dave. So they had phoned Bottomley Hall— they knew the number, since it turned out that their tent was pitched on Lord Rader-Wellorff's land— and Peevish had driven straight over with them.

Peevish had been less certain about playing Animal Car Wars, but Jeremy, Teremy, Meremy, Heremy, Queremy, Smellemy, Sea Anemone, and Dave had all insisted that they weren't going to chicken out of a challenge, otherwise they didn't deserve the name Rader-Wellorff.

Which was why the double-decker bus was now lined up in a starting position beside the Rolls-Royce limousine, the bus filled with cows (and one dog), the limo with sheep. Although cows were the bigger of the two animals, the limo looked more stuffed as it also had to fit Jeremy, Teremy, Meremy, Heremy, Queremy, Smellemy, Sea Anemone, and Dave (and Peevish, driving).

Elliott Cool got into the driver's seat of the bus, next to Barry.

"OK," said Barry. "You work the pedals and I'll do the steering wheel."

"Like, really?" said Elliott.

"Yes. My feet can't reach the pedals."

"Yes, I can see that. But I mean . . . really?"

"Well, it is exactly what I want . . . ," said Barry.

"Like, OK . . . ?" said Elliott grimly and put his feet on the pedals.

"Rev, please," said Barry.

Elliott took a deep breath and revved the accelerator. To the side of them, the Rolls-Royce limo revved in reply.

Barry nodded toward Mama Cool standing in front, between the bus and the limo. She looked terrified, but raised her flag anyway—the spotty tablecloth fluttered for a second in the wind—and then brought it down.

CHAPTER SEVEN

"**H**it the accelerator!" said Barry. "Floor it!" Elliott did as he was told. The bus moved forward—very fast (for a bus).

"*Moo! Moo!!*" went the cows. "*Whimper slurp, whimper slurp,*" went Neil, which suggested quite strongly that he was frightened but comforting himself with occasional sips from the udder.

Barry looked over. Despite the bus's speed, it was still a bus, and the Rolls-Royce was still a car, and so it was getting ahead. He could see Jeremy, Teremy, Meremy, Heremy, Queremy, Smellemy, Sea Anemone, Dave, and a number of sheep sticking their heads out of the electric roof, waving scornfully at him. (The sheep weren't waving scornfully, they were just sticking their heads out, although one of them was going *Baa!* in what Barry took to be a mocking manner.)

"Faster!" said Barry.

"It won't, like, go any faster?! It's, like, a double-decker bus?!"

"*Moo!!*"

Barry tightened his hands around the wheel and turned it sharply toward the right. The front side of the bus banged against the back side of the limo. It knocked the limo off its path, spinning it around. And around and around and around, like a top.

"AAAAAAHHHH!!" Barry could hear faintly, under the roar of the bus engine.

And also: "BAAAAAAAAA!!"

"OK," said Barry. "While they're out of control
—head for the finish line!"

"Like, OK?!!!" said Elliott, who suddenly looked as if he was enjoying himself. He pressed down hard on the accelerator again.

The finish line was a trail of Mung Bean Muck-Muck that Barry had made Mama Cool drip out with a spoon. They went past it easily. Barry looked behind: the limo had ended up marooned in the middle of the field.

"Hooray! We've won!" said Barry.

"Hey . . . ," said Elliott. "Cool!"

"OK!" said Barry. "Now, hit the brakes!"

"I am!" said Elliott.

"Harder!"

"I'm, like, pressing down as hard as I can?!"

They looked through the windshield. Rushing toward them was the cliff edge and, beyond that, the sea.

"Why won't the brakes work?!" screamed Barry.

"I think a combination of going too fast, hitting the limousine, and getting the wheels covered in Muck-Muck means we can't, like, stop?!?!" screamed Elliott.

"Moo!!!"

"Whimper whimper whimper slurrrppp!!"

"Oh my God!!" shouted Barry. "Come on, Elliott . . . don't lose your cool!!"

"I've lost it, man! Completely, like, gone?!! THIS IS, LIKE, NOT COOOOOOOL?!!"

"Moooooooooooooo!!!"

"Not *coooooooool*!!!"

They were skidding closer and closer to the edge. Barry looked around. Mama Cool was chasing after them, waving her arms, perhaps in the hope of creating enough wind to suck them back. Behind her, Peevish, Jeremy, Teremy, Meremy, Heremy, Queremy, Smellemy, Sea Anemone, Dave, and the sheep had got out of the limo and were pointing at them. (None of the sheep were pointing, but they were watching.)

Even Lord Rader-Wellorff had arrived to see what was happening. And, beyond him, Barry thought he saw two other faces—that man, and that woman—looking at him. The ones he'd seen at Bottomley Hall and the after-party with Vlassorina and the soccer match. As their faces receded away from him at some speed, he couldn't see them properly, but could somehow make out their expressions, of concern and hope and . . . something else.

But before Barry could screw up his eyes to try and see them more clearly, Elliott screamed again. Barry turned around. All he could see was the oncoming cliff edge.

CHAPTER EIGHT

Barry shut his eyes. Then, as they lurched forward, he heard an enormous scrunching *clunk*.

What was odd about this enormous scrunching *clunk* was that it didn't come, as Barry had expected, with terrible pain and broken bones and drowning and death. It just came with a jolt.

On that basis, he opened his eyes to discover that the bus had been stopped by some unseen object about ten meters from the cliff edge.

There was a banging sound to his left. He looked over. It was Mama Cool, looking, it has to be said, not at all cool, pounding on the window. Barry opened the door.

"Our tent!" she cried. "Our beautiful tent!"

"What's happened to it?" said Barry.

"It's under the [   ] bus!"

Actually, she said a swear here. A BIG swear. Before the word bus. But Barry decided to tune that out and pretend he hadn't heard it.

"Oh," he said. "I'm really sorry . . . ."

"That's not good enough!"

Barry thought. "I'm really . . . like, sorry?" he said.

Judging from her expression, that didn't help, either. He opened the door and came down from the driver's cab. Elliott followed him, looking more than slightly dazed. Mama Cool started pulling a corner of tent tarpaulin that was sticking out from under the front wheel. She pulled it hard. It broke. She fell over.

Barry was starting to feel really sorry for the Cools by now. He was about to do a truly big apology when he heard a loud voice behind him.

"Mr. and Mrs. Cool!"

He turned round. It was Lord Rader-Wellorff, with Jeremy, Teremy—oh, you know, all of them—by his side.

Lord Rader-Wellorff was standing over Elliott and Mama Cool. He looked very upset. "You are tenants on my land. And you have put my children at terrible risk! To say nothing of what you've done to my Rolls-Royce limousine! What have you got to say for yourselves . . . ?!"

Elliott and Mama Cool looked up, shamefaced. They just held each other's hands, not saying anything.

"In fact, do you have anything to say before I instruct Peevish to have you thrown orff my land immediately?!"

Barry decided it was time for him to speak. It was time for him to explain that none of this was Elliott and Mama Cool's fault—well, except insofar as they had told him to do exactly what he liked—but never mind about that. *Basically, the point is you should be blaming me, Lord Rader-Wellorff, not them.* That was what he needed to say.

Barry stepped forward, in between Lord Rader-Wellorff and Elliott and Mama Cool. He opened his mouth. Unfortunately, just at that point, his stomach started to rumble. Really rumble. Inside his intestines, the A-Bombs had been mixing with the Sugar Sugars and the Banana Balls and the Caramel Hi-Kools and the Toffee Snakes and, perhaps worst of all, the spoonful of Mung Bean Muck-Muck he'd eaten earlier. And then it had all been shaken about in a very bumpy trip across the field in a skidding, out-of-control double-decker bus.

He put his hand on his tummy. He opened his

mouth. And from his mouth came not an apology, but the most multicolored, sparkly stream of vomit anyone had ever seen. It was like a beautiful rainbow of vomit.

Luckily, Mama Cool had realized what was about to happen as soon as Barry put his hand on his tummy and heard the loud rumble. So, in the nick of time, pulling Elliott with her, she jumped in front of Barry so that she and her husband could act as a human shield for Lord Rader-Wellorff.

Unluckily, this did mean that she and Elliott ended up covered head to foot in Barry's beautiful rainbow of vomit.

"Oh! Oh! Oh!" said Lord Rader-Wellorff, backing away.

Jeremy, Teremy, Meremy, Queremy, and all the rest of them backed off as well, going, "Urrggh!! Urggh!!!"

The rainbow went on for a long time. Barry made a strange noise throughout, which made the cows, who were still on the bus, look over with interest, thinking that perhaps he too was a cow.

Finally, it stopped. In the Bible, there's a story about Lot's wife, who God turns into a pillar of salt. The final scene here was a bit like that except, instead of Lot's wife, it was Elliott and Mama Cool and, instead of God, it was Barry Bennett and, instead of salt, it was vomit.

"Ahem," said Lord Rader-Wellorff, stepping forward, but not too far forward. "Well. That was unfortunate. But, I have to say, very good of you, Mr. and Mrs. Cool, to . . . step into the firing line, as it were. Very good indeed. To get in the way of all that . . ."

He waved his hand toward what they were covered in.

"Vomit!"

"Yaahs, thank you, Jeremy. So, in view of that, let's just forget all about that business with the bus and the children and the Rolls-Royce limousine and throwing you orff my land. As you were," he said. "Jolly good! Peevish! Children! Time to go!"

With that, he turned away. Barry looked up at Mama and Elliott Cool. He could just make out their eyes, in between drippy globs of red and green and orange. They were staring at him blankly.

"No, Dave, I know it smells of candy, but you can't go and lick it orff them . . ." he heard Lord Rader-Wellorff say in the distance. But that didn't distract Barry. He'd made up his mind.

"Please, Barry . . . ," said Mama Cool.

"Yes, please, Barry . . . ," said Elliott.

Barry knew what they were going to say: *Be our son.* And he was going to say yes. *He was going to say yes.*

". . . can you go back to the Parent Agency. AS SOON AS POSSIBLE!!"

"Oh," said Barry.

FRIDAY

CHAPTER ONE

"Oh dear . . . ," said the Head. "Is everything all right now?"

"Yes," said Barry. "Lord Rader-Wellorff gave them some money for a new tent. And said they could stay on his land for as long as they liked . . ."

"Oh well, that's good."

"And he even got Peevish to bring down a big hose to their field to wash off all the vomit."

The Head looked a little queasy at this.

"Couldn't they have just jumped in the sea?" said Secretary One.

"I'm not sure all those chemicals would be good for the environment," said Secretary Two.

"Yes, well, let's not talk about it anymore," said the Head, who had turned a strange shade of green. "So, Barry . . . you've got one more go at it . . ." He turned over the last 24-Hourglass, the red one. "Better make it count," he said.

Barry wanted to ask why. What *happens* if it doesn't work out with the next set of parents either? But he knew that no one would answer this question. They would just mutter darkly and change the subject. Which meant all Barry knew was that what would happen was probably really, really bad.

He took out, for the last time, his list. It was EXTREMELY crumpled by now. He scanned it quickly. He knew it very well, having read it, it seemed, a million times since he'd been in this world. Being boring—check; not being famous—check; being poor—check; not letting him play video games— well, he hadn't done that one . . . but he didn't think it was enough to say "parents who will let me play video games." That should have been the Cools with their whole let-him-do-anything attitude, but they didn't *have* any video games—or any electricity— and then he saw it, marked as if to remind him by a little splash of rainbow vomit.

Number 7: "Being always <u>much</u> nicer to ~~my twin sisters~~ TSE than to me . . ."

"I'd like to try out parents . . . where I'm the favorite child, please."

"Write that down, Secretary Two!" said Secretary One.

"I'm writing it down, Secretary One!" said Secretary Two, her pad already flipped over and halfway through writing down the word FAVORITE (FAVO she'd written so far).

"OK . . . ," said the Head, opening his laptop. "So we're back to parents with other children then. Because there's not much point in being the favorite if you're the only child, eh?"

"Write that down as well!" said Secretary One.

"I'm writing it down!" said Secretary Two, furiously scribbling the words OTHER CHILDREN.

While they were doing that, Barry had a thought. Number 7 was on his list because of the way he felt things were in his family. Because of the way his parents were when it came to him and his sisters. Now The Secretary Entity weren't exactly The Sisterly Entity, but they were pretty close. And so Barry said:

"Actually . . . what about . . . ?" He gestured with his head to his left.

"What . . . ?" said the Head. He looked over. "Well. That's not a bad idea. Secretaries!"

They both stopped writing and looked up.

"You'll be all right if Barry spends his last day with *your* parents, won't you?"

Both of them looked at him openmouthed. Neither of them wrote down the words OUR PARENTS.

CHAPTER TWO

On the way to The Secretary Entity's house—they walked there, as it was only around the corner from the Parent Agency—the two girls were clearly annoyed with Barry.

"Well, Barry, I mean I understand why you might want this, but I really think . . . ," one of them was saying.

"And I think too . . . ," said the other one.

". . . that you've chosen the wrong parents."

"Yes, our parents . . ."

"Marjorie and Malcolm Bustle . . ."

"Yes, Marjorie and Malcolm Bustle . . ."

"They are *very* solicitous with us."

"Solicitous means caring. Looking after. Not neglecting."

Barry nodded as if he'd known that. He hadn't.

"I mean, for example, every time our daddy . . ."

"Malcolm Bustle."

"Yes, Malcolm Bustle—every time he sees us, he picks us up, whirls us around, and gives us a kiss."

"Yes he does."

Barry nodded again.

"So I just can't see any way that they're going to fulfill your requirements in this particular case."

"No, I don't see it either."

"Perhaps the Head should have suggested some other ones."

"Yes, perhaps he should."

By now, they were at The Secretary Entity's house. It was a nice-looking house: considerably nicer than the one The *Sisterly* Entity lived in, thought Barry. He looked around. The road it faced was leafy and quiet, with no sign of any big trucks making the houses shake.

Secretary One pressed on the button to the side of the front door.

"Hello?" said a voice.

"Dad?" said Secretary One.

"It's us!!" said Secretary Two.

A man who looked a bit like one of The Secretary Entity—only much taller, and older, and male—opened the door. The Secretary Entity drew themselves up to their full height, ready to be picked up, whirled about, and kissed.

"Barry!!! Hello, Barry!!! We're so pleased to see you, Barry!!" said Malcolm Bustle, picking him up, whirling him around, and giving him a kiss on the cheek.

"Barry! Barry! Barry! Barry! Barry! Barry! Barry!" said Marjorie Bustle (who looked like The Secretary Entity too, only taller, and older, and female), appearing behind her husband and opening her arms wide. And adding one more "Barry!" just in case.

"Nice to meet you, Malcolm and Marjorie," said Barry, as Malcolm set him down.

"Hello, Mom!" said Secretary One.

"Hello, Dad!" said Secretary Two.

"Do come in, Barry," said Malcolm. Barry went through the door.

Which Marjorie then shut, leaving The Secretary Entity on the doorstep.

"So, Barry," said Marjorie. "Lovely to meet you. I—"

There was a *tap-tap-tap* noise from behind them. They looked around. The mail slot was flapping up and down. Then it flapped up and stayed there.

Barry could just about see two pairs of little-girl eyes peeping through the slot.

"Mom?"

"Dad?"

"Um . . . you seem . . . ha-ha . . . to have locked us out . . ."

"Accidentally, of course!"

"Oh yes, of course."

"Barry?" said Marjorie. "Sorry to bother you, but . . . can you hear a noise?"

"Hmm . . . ," said Barry. "You mean a kind of . . . annoying buzzing sound? Like some trapped flies?"

"Um . . . yes," said Malcolm.

"Oh!" said Barry. "I think it might be these two." He opened the door again. The Secretary Entity were standing on the doorstep, smiling and waving.

"Hi, Mom!"

"Hi, Dad!"

Malcolm and Marjorie didn't say anything in reply.

CHAPTER THREE

Barry looked around the Bustles' living room. He had been expecting it—what with The Secretary Entity being a version of The Sisterly Entity—to be more like his own living room at home.

At home, his family did their weekly shop at Morrisons. But on their way to it they passed Waitrose. Barry would see parents in there, shopping with their children. He didn't know any of those children, and hadn't been in any of their living rooms, but he imagined that, if he had, they would look like this one. And smell like it—of fresh bread and coffee. And sound like it—in the background, he could hear a serious voice on the radio discussing "the glass ceiling in the banking sector," whatever that was.

The floor was wooden and polished. There was a fireplace with a rug in front of it. At the other end of the living room, it became a kitchen. On the walls, there were some modern art paintings and also lots of certificates won by The Secretary Entity: Best Dressed, Best Spoken, and (there were *loads* of these) Best Handwriting.

Also on the walls were four big canvas pictures of The Secretary Entity, from when they were babies to now. But Malcolm was presently taking those down and putting up four big canvas pictures of Barry.

"I hope you like these," he was saying. The girls came in, frowning hard at their father. "I had them made up from a photo they sent from the Agency." He stepped back to look at the pictures. "All the same photograph, of course, but I tinted them with different colors. What do you think?"

"Lovely," said Barry.

"What have you done to *our mom and dad*?" hissed Secretary One to Barry.

"Oh," said Barry quietly. "Not much . . ."

"How much is not much?" said Secretary Two, also hissing.

"Just asked the Head to have a little word with your parents before we got here, explaining how I'd like it all to work . . . *if they wanted me to choose them in the end . . .*"

The Secretary Entity looked at each other, open-mouthed. Then Secretary One turned to Barry and said: "I can't believe our beloved mother and father are actually going to go along with such a disg—"

"Barry!!" called Marjorie from the kitchen bit of

the room. "What would you like for lunch?"

"Hmm," said Barry. "Pizza?"

"Oh well, you've made a mistake there," said Secretary One smugly. "We only ever eat gluten-free, free-range, nut-free, chemical-free, salt-and-sugar-free food."

"Yes, our food is very, very free," said Secretary Two. "Except, of course, it costs a lot of money."

"But we never, *ever, ever* eat junk food."

"Yes, our parents would simply never allow it."

"So . . . ," said Marjorie, coming out from the kitchen holding a takeout menu from somewhere called *Pizza Shed*, "what would you like: *Ten Cheese? Crispy Hottie? Latino? Old 'n' New? Salty Bananas? Fifty Fish? German? Meat Meat Meat? String? Nobody Likes This One? Eggy Norman?*"

"What's *Eggy Norman?*"

"Er . . . mozzarella, bacon, tuna, pickled cucumbers, tomatoes, pineapple, and then, in the middle, a hard-boiled egg carved into the shape of a small man called Norman."

"I'll have a *Ten Cheese*," said Barry after a moment's thought.

"I'll call them straight away," said Marjorie, picking up the phone.

"*Mom!*" said Secretary One.

"What?" said Marjorie. "I love . . . pizza."

"What do you love about it?" said Secretary Two.

Marjorie looked a little uncomfortable. "The . . . cheese. And the grease . . . And the salt. And the big fatty . . . bread." She stared at the menu for quite a long time. "Yum," she said eventually. Very quietly.

"But . . . ," said Secretary One, "what are *we* going to have?"

"Pizza, of course," said Barry.

Marjorie looked at him. He held her gaze. She seemed to sigh, then looked at The Secretary Entity. "If it's good enough for Barry, it's good enough for you."

"You don't have to order them anything," said Barry. "They can have my bits of crust. I don't eat those."

"Perfect," said Marjorie, dialing the number for *Pizza Shed*.

The Secretary Entity looked on, amazed.

Malcolm appeared, coming down the stairs.

"Do you have any video games?" said Barry.

Malcolm frowned and went back up.

"No!" screamed Secretary One. "Of course we don't!"

"We only watch educational and improving television!" screamed Secretary Two.

"So don't expect any of that garbage here, I'm afr—"

"Yes, Barry, I think I got everything you wanted. . . ." They turned around to see Malcolm coming downstairs again, his arms overflowing with small boxes. "I've already set up the TV with a Flii and a Ybox, and

you can play any of these: *Spanky's Quest*; *Ninja Zebra*;
Space Pitch 'n' Putt; *Find the Fat Tongue*; *Zombie Crash 3*;
Death in the Car: The Game; *Monkey Sticks*; *Boxers vs.
Spear-throwers*; *Psyborg 2014*; *Seven Second Soccer Sevens*;
Marble Man; *Stinky Pirate Revenge . . .*"

"I think *Stinky Pirate Revenge* only works on the
Flii . . . ," said Barry, looking at the cover.

"Right, OK. I'll bear that in mind," said Malcolm.
"So! TV on . . ."

"Dad! We want to watch *Masterbrain!*"

"Yes! And *University Big Clevers*! And *Come Read
With Me!*"

Malcolm glanced at Barry and also, like Marjorie
had before, seemed to sigh. "Yes. Well. You can
watch them another day." He went over to the TV and
switched the game console on. "For now, Barry—fill
your boots!"

Barry looked at his shoes. Then he remembered
what that expression meant.

"Thanks!" he said, sitting down with the Flii control. On the TV, a cartoon pirate appeared, covered in what appeared to be bits of old food. "Oo-er, me hearties! I am SmellyBeard, terror of the seven seas!" he said. "Think ye I whiff? Well then . . ." He drew his curved sword. "I SHALL HAVE ME REVENGE!!"

"Thanks . . . Dad . . . ?" suggested Malcolm tentatively.

"Maybe," said Barry, pressing the buttons on the controller expertly.

CHAPTER FOUR

Barry had a great afternoon. He played *Stinky Pirate Revenge* right up to the end. He only stopped playing to have lunch, which was also great: the *Ten Cheese* pizza was fantastic. He also really liked the *Eggy Norman*, which Malcolm ordered, and then let Barry eat Norman himself, who had an egg hat and a yolk tie.

The Secretary Entity, however, did not have such a great afternoon. They stared in disbelief as Barry actually did pop his pizza crusts onto their empty plates. They stared in even more disbelief as both their parents sat on the sofa watching while Barry and his Flii controller made SmellyBeard walk the plank off his pirate ship, and when SmellyBeard fell in the water—which turned out to be an enormous toilet sailing beside his ship—Malcolm and Marjorie clapped! And Marjorie said: "Oh, Barry! You're such a clever boy!"

But they saved their *most* disbelieving stares for when Malcolm and Marjorie came to them, later in the afternoon, with the plans for Barry's birthday party.

"We love you, Barry, we do . . . We love you, Barry, we do . . . We love you, Barry, dear *Baaarry* . . ."

Malcolm and Marjorie held the note the longest; The Secretary Entity held it quite a lot shorter, but then it was hard to sing anything through gritted teeth.

"We love you, Barry—we do!"

Malcolm and Marjorie clapped and cheered. Meanwhile, The Secretary Entity presented Barry with his cake. As directed by Barry on his plans, this involved both of them kneeling on one knee, on either side of the cake, and then handing it up to him.

The cake was a chocolate one. On top of it, also in accordance with the plans, it said, in strawberry icing: TO BARRY—THE BEST. Barry had thought about having them add CHILD IN THIS HOUSE but eventually decided that just THE BEST was cooler. And, judging by the expressions on their faces as they handed over the cake, it was still having the same effect on The Secretary Entity. Which was the point.

"Oh, I'm *so* glad I decided to go for a party at home this time. It's been a very tiring week," said Barry, leaning over, ready to blow out the ten candles.

He took a deep breath and brought his lips close to the cake.

The Secretary Entity glanced at each other. Then, suddenly, they put their faces close to the cake too and, using their combined breath, blew out every single one of the candles before Barry had a chance to.

Barry looked up at Malcolm and Marjorie with a hurt expression on his face.

"Girls! How *dare* you!" said Marjorie.

"Yes!" said Malcolm. "That's a terrible thing to do to Barry!!"

"But that's what you *told* us to do!" said Secretary One.

"Yes," said Secretary Two, "you said we *had* to do it, because *he's* the one who normally gets punished and so he wanted to see someone *else* get it in the neck for a—"

"Shhhhh!!!" said Malcolm with an anxious glance over at Barry. "You're spoiling it."

"Yes," said Marjorie. "Could you stick to your lines, please?"

The Secretary Entity looked very tired.

"OK, whatever," said Secretary One. "Ha-ha-ha, we hate you, Barry, that's why we blew out your candles . . . ," she continued in a bored voice.

"Yes, we just want to ruin your party because we're very, very selfish and annoying," said Secretary Two in an equally bored voice.

"Right!" said Malcolm. "Exactly! So! Go to your room!"

"Yes, to your room! With no cake!" said Marjorie.

"Hold on a minute," said Barry, raising his arm.

"Yes, what is it, darling?" said Marjorie.

Barry stood up. He looked at The Secretary Entity. "I think they should be allowed a slice of cake each before they go. . . ."

"Well, that's very, very generous of you, Barry, isn't it, girls?" said Malcolm.

"Seriously?" said Secretary One. Marjorie just gave her a look. "OK, yes, it's very generous . . . ," she said in a let's-just-get-this-over-with way.

"Yes, very generous," said Secretary Two in exactly the same way.

"Here you are," said Barry, who had sliced two sections of cake. He handed a plate to each of them.

"Say thank you to Barry," said Marjorie.

"Thank you, Barry," said The Secretary Entity in their bored voice.

"Don't mention it," said Barry, handing over two forks.

"Is it a vegan cake, Mommy?" said Secretary One.

"Yes, sugar-, nut- and indeed chocolate-free?" said Secretary Two.

"Er . . . ," said Marjorie Bustle, looking at the cake awkwardly, ". . . no."

"Barry...he doesn't like those ones," said Malcolm, even more awkwardly.

The Secretary Entity stared at the cake like they would normally turn their noses up at it. But, then again, they had only had some pizza crusts for lunch; so after a second they dived in and started eating.

Suddenly, both of their faces contorted.

"*Urrrrgghhhh!!*" said one.

"*Fwurrggggghhh!!*" said the other.

"What's the matter?" said Malcolm.

It was hard for either of them to speak as their mouths were full of cake. But Secretary One managed to say, through what looked like a mouthful of mud: "It's got SALT IN IT!!"

"Not *in* it," said Barry. "*On* it . . ." He held up a salt shaker. And smiled.

"And . . . *ugggrrggh*!! Pepper!"

Barry held up the pepper grinder. "Yes. Sorry."

Malcolm and Marjorie glanced at each other.

"*Fwurrggggghhh!!*" said Secretary Two, spitting crumbs of cake out onto the floor.

Malcolm and Marjorie continued to look at each other. Then Marjorie leaned over to Malcolm and whispered, very quietly: "I don't know how much more of this I can stand . . . ."

"I know," whispered Malcolm back. "But . . . what else can we do?"

"Give up on the idea of a third child?"

"Is that what you want?"

She thought for a second then shook her head.

"OK," said Malcolm, still whispering. "So, for the moment . . . *just go with it*, Marjorie!"

She nodded. They turned, together.

"Ha-ha-ha!!" said Malcolm. "What a funny joke, Barry!"

"Yes!" said Marjorie. "That's one of the funniest practical jokes I've ever seen! You're so funny and clever!"

Barry was about to smile and say "Thank you" when The Secretary Entity started making some very strange noises. Not just *"Fwurrgggghhh!!"* but also *"Crrgggghh!!"* and *"Kkkkkracchhh!!"*

Then Secretary One fell to the floor, clutching her throat.

Followed almost immediately by Secretary Two, doing the same.

CHAPTER FIVE

"**U**m . . . are they OK?" said Marjorie.

"Yes, yes, fine. Aren't you, girls?" said Malcolm.

"*Urggghblarrp!!*" said Secretary One.

"*Dszssefffccch!*" said Secretary Two.

"There you are," said Malcolm.

Now for Barry, up to this point, all of this had, in a way, been fun. Even though The Secretary Entity weren't exactly The Sisterly Entity, they were enough like them—in terms of looking and acting just the same—for Barry to really enjoy getting his own back for once. And it had felt nice, knowing that the grown-ups were always going to take his side, however badly he behaved.

At the same time, it had *also* felt a little bit . . . nasty. And, as the day had gone on, he had found that the thrill of being the favorite—and being able to do things that he knew would get under The Secretary Entity's skin—had got less and less, and the feeling of nastiness had grown. It was almost as if he had to get nastier and nastier to feel the same thrill again.

Watching both sisters writhe on the floor—Secretary One had gone blue and Secretary Two purple—*should* have felt great, because that's why he'd chosen this type of parent and drawn up a big plan for how they had to be: so that he could feel what it would be like to take revenge on his little sisters. And what was better than this? Barry had, after all, in his darkest moments wished one or both of his sisters were dead.

But it didn't feel great. It felt awful.

And seeing Malcolm and Marjorie stand by while it was happening because they didn't want to upset Barry—because they thought that's what he wanted them to do—felt even worse.

So Barry stepped forward and said: "Time for the Grübenschnitzel Maneuver!!"

"Pardon?" said Malcolm.

"Um . . . even though you are our favorite, Barry," said Marjorie, "I don't think now is the best time for *more* food . . ."

"No!" said Barry. "The Grübenschnitzel Maneuver!!"

Remembering exactly what Derek *Fwahm!* had done to him, he bent down quickly to Secretary One. He grabbed her by the heels in order to pick her up and turn her upside down. But he only succeeded in dragging her legs halfway up his own body. Then he tried to do the same to Secretary Two, but her legs kept falling back down again.

Eventually, he managed to get both of them on either side of him with their legs sort of up against his sides. He raised his arms in order to slap them hard on the back in the correct Grübenschnitzel manner. But all he could manage from this position was a light tap on each of their bottoms, which was both useless and not a little embarrassing.

By now, The Secretary Entity had started making noises that couldn't even be written down. Barry looked over to Malcolm and Marjorie to help. But they seemed rooted to the spot with terror. Barry turned back toward the floor. He felt a huge swell of emotion building up in him. The thought of The Secretary Entity choking, or being really hurt in any way, seemed suddenly like the worst thing possible.

Barry realized there was something he needed to say. It was really just two words. But he hadn't said them for a very long time. He didn't even know if they were the right words in this strange, like-his-but-not-exactly-like-his-world world. But there was nothing else left to do.

"GINNY!!" he said. "KAY!! Breathe!! Please!! Breathe!!"

Even from their half-upside-down position—even while choking, even about to fall into unconsciousness—both little girls looked very surprised at this. So surprised, in fact, that both of them stuck their heads up and looked at Barry and, in doing so, coughed violently, ejecting—like little spongy cannonballs from their throats—the pesky bits of salty, peppery cake that had been lodged there.

Both of these bits of cake (quite sloppy and messy by now) curved up in the air and hit Barry—*splodge!*—simultaneously on each cheek.

Immediately, Malcolm and Marjorie rushed to

hug Kay and Ginny. As Barry watched the two girls being folded in their parents' arms, he realized something: *most parents didn't have favorites among their children.* They loved all their children, in different ways, at different times. And it didn't matter if sometimes that wasn't you, because soon it would be. And also that it was OK—no, it was nice, it was good—to see your sisters loved.

As it happened, after he'd had this deep and meaningful realization about how it didn't matter about being a family favorite, he became this family's favorite. Marjorie looked around from hugging the girls and said: "Oh, Barry! Thank you, Barry!"

"Yes! Thank you, Barry!" said Malcolm.

"Actually, yes, thank you very much, Barry . . . ," said Secretary One.

"Me too with the thanks, Barry!" said Secretary Two.

And then they all came over and hugged him.

Which was lovely. Although Barry did feel, in the middle of it, suddenly very, very tired.

"But how did you know our names?" Secretary One was saying. "We've never told you them . . ."

Barry just smiled wearily and said: "I'm going back to the Parent Agency."

FRIDAY NIGHT

CHAPTER ONE

"**S**o, Barry," said the Head. "You've had your five days with five parents but now it's decision time. Which of the five sets of parents would you like to choose?"

"Um . . . when you say choose . . . you mean go and live with forever . . . ?" said Barry.

"Yes!" said the Head. "Until you grow up, of course. And then you'll have to come and see us to apply for children. It won't be me in this chair by then, I shouldn't think. . . . Ha-ha!"

The Head looked to The Secretary Entity to laugh at his joke. But they just looked pained.

"Are you all right, Secretary One?"

"I'm fine, thank you, Head," said Secretary One.

"You sound a little throaty."

"I'm also fine, thank you, Head," said Secretary Two.

"So do you actually."

Barry looked out of the window. It was late on Friday night—they had kept the Agency open for him specially—and the lights of the city were glittering outside.

"I don't know," said Barry. He looked down at his list, which was lying on his lap. It was so crumpled now that even he couldn't really read it, although he was the one who had written it.

"Hmm," said the Head. "I'm afraid you really have to make your mind up now." He looked over at the last 24-Hourglass, the red one. It had about a hundred grains of sand left. One went through. Then another. "It's nearly midnight. And past midnight, you'll be ten. And then . . ."

He trailed off. As usual.

Suddenly, Barry felt very angry with him. "What?" he said, loudly and sharply.

The Head raised an eyebrow. Not a big one, just a standard up-it-goes. "Pardon?"

Barry took a deep breath. "Then—what?! Every time I come back here, there's always a moment where you and them"—he did a thumb gesture toward The Secretary Entity—"go quiet about what happens to children who get to ten without finding parents! But now I want to know! I have to!"

The Head sighed. He got up and went to the window—the one with the amazing view of the city—and looked out, not saying anything. He had his back to Barry. He opened the window. Then he turned around. His face looked white with dread.

"OK, Barry. This is what happens to children who don't find parents by the age of ten. Basically—"

As he said this, a powerful gust of wind came into the room and blew Barry's list up into the air.

"Oh my God!" said Barry.

The piece of paper was lifted by the wind, high up to the ceiling, toward the open window. The four of them—Barry and The Secretary Entity and the Head—jumped up, trying to catch it, but because they were, after all, just children, they were too small.

Plus, the list was so crumpled now it had formed lots of little folds and crinkles which acted as tiny wings. And so it continued to float above the jumping children, and then another gust caught it and it flew beyond their grasping hands and out of the window.

"Oh! Oh! Oh!" said the Head. "I'm very sorry, Barry. I really am. Shall we send PCs 890 and 891 out to look for it?"

Barry sighed and sat down again. "No, it's OK. I guess it doesn't matter anymore . . . ."

The Head and The Secretary Entity sat down too, looking rather uncertain as to what to say next. Instinctively, they all looked to the 24-Hourglass. Now there were about seventy grains left.

Then sixty-nine.

"So," said the Head. "What were we talking about?"

"Barry's parental choice, sir . . . ," said Secretary One.

"Of course!" said the Head. "So. Barry. Which couple do you like best . . . ?"

Barry stared at him. He shook his head. Clearly, he was never going to find out exactly what happened to children who didn't find parents they liked by the time they were ten. But it was obviously something not very nice. So he said: "Well . . . there is a couple . . ."

"Splendid. The Rader-Wellorffs? Vlassorina? The *Fwahms!*? Elliott and Mama Cool? Malcolm and—?"

"Um . . . well . . ." Barry leaned over the Head's desk. The Head leaned over toward him. "Not exactly. I was wondering about this *other* couple—this man and woman. I keep on seeing them wherever I go. Not the whole time. Just in moments."

The Head leaned back. "Well, do you know who they are . . . ?"

Barry frowned. "When I first saw them, their faces looked blurry. But each time I've seen them again, they've gotten slightly clearer."

The Head glanced at The Secretary Entity, who shrugged. "Are they on our books?" he said.

"Yes," said Barry. "I think so. I mean, I thought I saw them when you first showed me some Parent Profiles, but it was so quick I'm not sure now."

"Well, let's have a look . . . ."

The Head flipped up the top of his gold laptop

and expertly brought up a series of Parent Files. He scrolled through them quickly. There were a few faces Barry recognized, but that was because they belonged to the parents he'd been trying out. Lord Rader-Wellorff's photo had him standing on a rug that was also a dead bear; Vlassorina was in black and white, and neither of them was looking at the camera. But there was no sign of the parents he was looking for.

"No," said Barry. "They're not there."

"Hmm," said the Head. "Well. Can you describe them?"

Barry thought. "Um . . . they look . . . kind. Although some of the time they look frightened. And something else. I don't know what it is. Their faces. They look at me with some . . . thing . . . something I can't quite name . . ."

The Head seemed to get a bit distracted during this speech from Barry. He drummed his fingers on the desk and looked anxiously at the 24-Hourglass.

It was hard to tell, but if you were someone with a magic gift for knowing, just by looking, how many things there were in one place—like, say, sweets in a jar at a fête—you'd have known that there were fifty-four grains left.

"Well, I'm afraid that very descriptive description won't be enough to pinpoint them among the millions of parents we have on file, I'm afraid. And time marches on! As we know, it's nearly . . ." He tapped the 24-Hourglass, which unfortunately had the effect of making the sand grains run down even quicker. ". . . your actual birthday."

This took Barry aback. He'd had so many different and weird parties this week, he'd forgotten.

His actual birthday. His real birthday.

"Yes . . ."

"Look, Barry. I like you. I feel you've become my personal responsibility. I'm not having you ending up . . . you know . . ."

Barry didn't know. But he wasn't going to start that again. There wasn't time and, besides, he did know that when the Head said "you know" The Secretary Entity shut their eyes and gulped. Which couldn't be good.

"So, if you can't decide, I'm afraid that means only one thing . . ."

"What?" said Barry, a bad feeling creeping up the back of his neck.

The Head looked him straight in the eye. "Code Black," he said and then pressed a button on the machine in the center of his desk.

CHAPTER TWO

Barry heard a mechanical swishing noise and looked to his right. The wall of the Head's office was sliding away to reveal, behind it: Lord and Lady Rader-Wellorff; Vlassorina; the *Fwahms!*; Elliott and Mama Cool; and Malcolm and Marjorie Bustle.

"Barrington!"

"Barrissina!"

"Barry!!!!"

"Like, Barry?!"

"Barry!"

"Oh no . . . ," said Barry.

They all came at him at once. The *Fwahms!* obviously got there first—*Fwahm! Fwahm!*—grabbing his right arm. The Rader-Wellorffs got to him next, Lady Rader-Wellorff's hat, with its model of Bottomley Hall, falling off in her hurry to get to his left arm. Vlassorina was next, Vlad doing a Dirk Large stunt leap to fasten a hand on to his right leg. It took Malcolm and Marjorie Bustle a little longer to reach his left leg, possibly because they were avoiding the accusing stares of The Secretary Entity.

Last up were Elliott and Mama Cool, who shambled up uncertainly and, realizing that Barry had no limbs left to grasp, put their hands on his head and shut their eyes and said, for some reason: "OMMMMM."

"What are *you* doing here?" said Barry, stopping their OMMMM before it had really got started. "I thought you didn't want me anyway."

"We've, like, changed our minds?" said Elliott Cool.

"I haven't!" said Mama Cool.

"Shh!!" said Elliott.

"Right. Well, what about you?" Barry said to Vlassorina, who were looking up at him from the ground. "I thought you found a girl to be your child! Patarina!"

"We put her on *The United Kid-Dom's Got Kids Who Do the Funniest Things*! And she won!" said Vlad.

"Singing a funny version of 'My Dog's Surprised by His Own Farts'!!! And now she's left us to pursue her career in Boysnia-Herzogeweeny!!!" said Morrissina.

"Oh . . . ," said Barry.

"Never mind them," said Lord Rader-Wellorff. "Come back to Bottomley Hall! We won't make you shoot any more birds!"

"Unless you want to!" said Lady Rader-Wellorff.

"No!" said Derek *Fwahm!* "Come and be with us!"

"We won't make you train too hard!" said Emily.

Although she was running on the spot as she said it, and Derek was doing a series of head-furtles.

"It's *us* you want to be with!" said Malcolm Bustle. "You'll be our favorite child!"

"He didn't like that, Malcolm. It made him feel bad!" said Marjorie.

"Oh yes! You *won't* be our favorite child!"

"No, that doesn't work either, you idiot!!"

Barry looked over at the Head. He felt, with all the parents holding on to him, like he was at the center of some weird gymnastic display.

The Head just shrugged his shoulders, pointed at the red 24-Hourglass—which must have had only about ten grains left in it—and said: "Gotta decide, Barry . . ."

At which point, all the parents just started pulling at him. His legs, his arms, his neck—every bit of his body was being pulled in a different direction.

"OW!!" screamed Barry. "You're hurting me!!" But none of the parents seemed to hear him, because

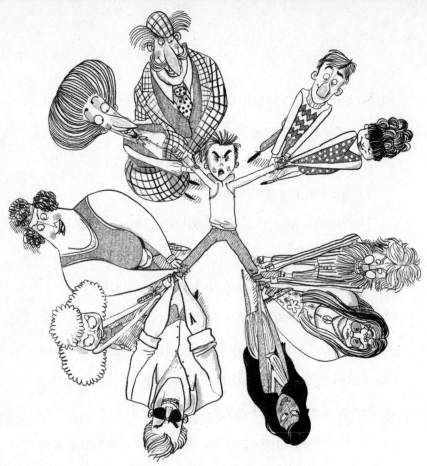

they were all shouting his name again.

"Please!" he screamed. "My arms! My legs! You're pulling them off!"

But they just carried on pulling and shouting, pulling and shouting. It really hurt. Barry felt as if he was going to faint. He whirled around, trying to get free, and *bang*! His body hit something, then he fell and cracked his head.

Everyone turned; the room was showered in rainbow-colored glass. *The 24-Hourglasses*, he thought dimly. *I must have knocked them over . . .*

The thought was never quite finished—a bit like how he imagined his grandpa's thoughts were these days. Instead, he could feel himself start to lose consciousness.

But just before he did so, just before his senses disappeared entirely, he had a moment of pure fear. A sense that, if he couldn't find parents that he liked, there was perhaps some deep black void, some horrible emptiness, waiting for him in this world. He felt he needed to stay awake and choose, somehow, someone, *anyone*, two people or one person, to be his parents, to look after him . . . or otherwise . . .

But now it was his turn, like the Head, to trail off . . .

. . . into the void.

BARRY! Barry!

BARRY! Barry! BARRY!

Barry! BARRY!

Barry! Barry!

Barry! Barry! Barry!

Barry!

Barry! Barry!

Barry! Barry!

Barry! Barry!

Barry! Barry! Barry!

Barry! Barry!

BARRY!

CHAPTER THREE

That was what woke him up, what pulled him out of the dark. His name being called.

At first, it just seemed to be the various parents shouting at him, trying to get him to come with them. But then Barry heard someone—a woman—saying his name much more softly . . . almost whispering it.

It broke his trance. He wasn't even sure he was in the Head's office anymore, but he could see, through the darkness, the couple. The man and woman he'd been trying to tell the Head about.

They were framed by a bright white light. It was so bright, Barry wanted to shut his eyes. But he could still see their faces looking at him. With concern. With hope. And with something else.

And now . . .

Now he knew what that something else was at last. He could see it in their eyes.

It was love.

And so he knew, finally, who they were.

"Mom! Dad!" he said.

PART THREE

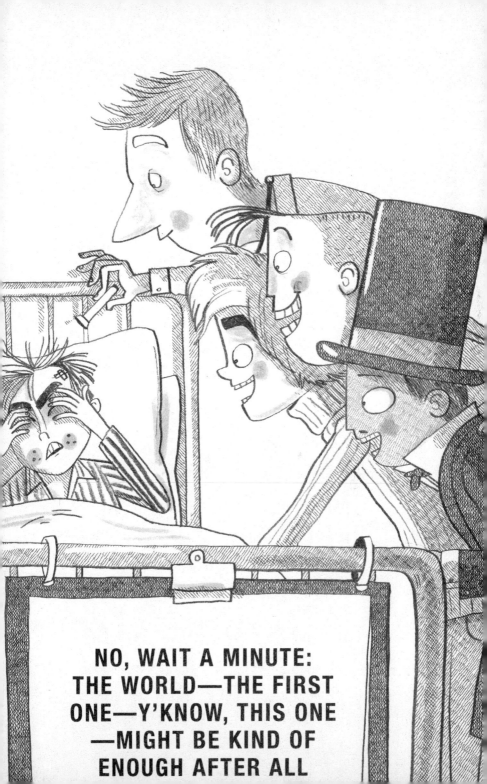

SATURDAY

CHAPTER ONE

At first, Barry couldn't understand where he was. He thought that perhaps he'd gone halfway back into his world and got stuck inside his bedroom wall, behind the poster of James Bond. Because, when the light in his eyes went away, standing in front of him was Q. He knew it was Q because he was wearing a tweed suit. It must have been him shining the light in his eyes, from a pen that was also an ultrapowerful laser.

Next to Q was a lady with a long dress and big 1960s hair, who seemed to be Miss Moneypenny. And, behind them, he could see lots of other characters—Jaws, and Oddjob, and that strange Spanish man with the blond wig from *Skyfall*. And he could hear, quite loudly, the theme music playing: Dah Da-Da-Da/Dadada/Dah!da-da-da/Da-Da-Da/DAH-DAH!/Dadada!!!

But then he realized it wasn't quite those people. It was people dressed up as them.

The man who looked like Q was his dad: Geoff Bennett. And the woman dressed as Miss Moneypenny was his mom: Susan Bennett.

"Barry!" said his mom, rushing forward. "Oh, Barry!" She bent over and hugged his head really tightly and kissed him over and over again. Which made it difficult to see what was going on. But he could just make out his dad's face. He was smiling, but also crying.

Why would he be doing that? And why were they dressed like this? And why, Barry thought, looking around him, was he—Barry—in some unfamiliar white bed?

A man appeared on the other side of the bed. Barry didn't recognize him, although he did look a little bit like Peevish/Jonty/Big Col. Only Peevish/Jonty/Big Col in a white coat.

His mom moved back to let this man speak to Barry, but she kept holding his hand.

"Hello, Barry," said the man. "I'm Dr. Evans."

"Hello . . . ," said Barry.

"Sorry about shining that light in your eyes just now."

"Oh. Was that you?"

"Yes," he said. "Do you know where you are?"

"The United Kid-Dom?" said Barry.

Dr. Evans frowned. "No . . . No. You're in a hospital. Off the A41 . . . Barry. Do you know what a coma is?"

Barry thought he did, but before he could answer, his dad spoke.

"Oh, Barry, I'm so sorry!! I'm so sorry I bought you the wrong *Casino Royale*!!"

That seemed so long ago Barry could hardly remember what his dad was talking about.

"Was it so bad it put me in a coma?" said Barry.

"What? No! No . . . ," said his dad. "No, it's just . . . after you threw it at Mom, we had that fight, and I sent you upstairs to bed. And then . . ." He stopped here and looked away.

"I ran out and upstairs to my room," said Barry.

"No, darling," said his mom. He looked over at her. "You tripped over."

"I did?"

"Yes. It was my fault. The dishwasher . . . you know how I always leave it open . . . ?"

"Yes."

"Well, it's because there's always so many dishes on the go, you know . . ."

"Yes . . ."

"Anyway, I was crouching there, not really looking because you'd thrown that DVD at me . . . and all my egg timers had fallen off the kitchen counter . . ."

"Oh yes! Sorry about that!"

"That's OK, my darling. But you were running so fast—and before I knew what had happened you'd slid on all the sand and glass on the floor. You landed on your head."

Now *she* looked away.

"And then . . ."

Barry looked up. It was one of The Sisterly Entity talking. They were dressed as Mr. Wint and Mr. Kidd, Blofeld's villainous henchmen from *Diamonds Are Forever*. Which meant they were both wearing men's suits and one of them had a fake mustache and glasses. This made Barry start to wonder which of the two worlds—this one or the United Kid-Dom—was real.

". . . then you just lay on the floor."

"Yes."

"Out cold."

"For ages."

"Well, until just now really."

"You've been in a coma for five days, Barry." This was Dr. Evans speaking.

Barry frowned. Five days? He sat up in bed. Jaws and Oddjob and the strange Spanish man with the wig from *Skyfall* were at the end of his bed.

"Hello!" said Jaws.

"Hi!" said Oddjob.

"Nice to have you back!" said the strange Spanish man with the wig from *Skyfall*.

Only it wasn't actually them: it was Lukas and Taj and Jake, dressed up. Jake's wig was even worse than the one in the film.

"Hello . . . ," said Barry. "But . . . why are you all here? And *why are you all dressed like this?"*

His dad nodded to his mom. His mom nodded to The Sisterly Entity. Who nodded to his friends. Who, as it turned out, were holding the music player that was playing the James Bond theme. Then all together—sort of half to the James Bond theme and half to the normal song—they sang:

"Happy Birthday to you, Happy Birthday to you, Happy Birthday, DEAR BAR-RY!! (that bit went with DA-DA!!) . . . Happy Birthday to you!!"

As the song ended, his mom produced a really big cake with ten candles surrounding some icing letters that said 007. Straddling the 0s, there was a little James Bond figure with a jet pack on.

"Barry . . . ," said his mom. "We've been sitting here every day and every night, hoping and praying that you'd come out of the coma. And then we thought: maybe he'll come around in time for his birthday. And, if he does, we thought . . ."

"We thought we should be ready to give you exactly the birthday party you wanted," said his dad. "Right here, if necessary." He bent down and, from a blue canvas IKEA bag, brought out, on a hanger, a child-size tuxedo.

"Oh wow!" said Barry.

"There's a gun to go with it!" said his dad, bending down again.

"Is it a real one?" said Barry.

"No," said his dad. He took out a black, solid-looking revolver. "But it is an exact replica of a Walther PPK."

"Oh!" said Barry. "That's amazing! Thank you so much!"

"Barry!" said one of The Sisterly Entity. "You've forgotten to blow out your candles!"

Barry turned to them. "Oh yes! Thanks for

reminding me, Ginny!"

Ginny looked confused at being called Ginny by her brother. Perhaps because it had been so long since he'd done so. "I'm Kay," she said.

"Oh, sorry. Sorry, Ginny," he said to the other one. "And thanks, Kay!"

And then, in one big blow, Barry blew out the candles. He blew so hard that the little James Bond, with his little jet pack, took off from the top of the cake. Which was just perfect.

CHAPTER TWO

Later, Barry had to have some tests done by Dr. Evans, but, after that, he was allowed to go home. He put on his tuxedo, and he and his mom and dad and his sisters went down in the elevator and out into the hospital parking lot. Parked there was the family's Ford Fiesta. His parents helped him put all his clothes and all the extra presents he'd got in the back.

Then his dad said: "OK, Susan, you take the girls home."

His mom nodded and got in the car. Ginny and Kay got in the back. They waved at him and shut the doors.

"Where are *we* going, Dad?" said Barry.

"We're going home too. We'll follow them."

"Right," said Barry, confused. The house was a long way away. "In what?"

His dad smiled at him.

"You know there was something else you wanted? You remember you said they weren't that expensive to rent . . ."

Barry nodded. He felt himself becoming really excited.

"Well, they are. *Very* expensive. So we couldn't rent one."

"Oh," said Barry and let the excitement drain out of him. His mom started up the Ford Fiesta.

"But it turns out that Jake's dad is a member of something called the Classic Car Club. *And* he let us borrow his membership for today. So . . ."

The Ford Fiesta moved out of its space. Revealing, behind it, a gleaming silver Aston Martin DB6.

Barry didn't know what to say. He just stared and stared at the beautiful car.

Suddenly, his dad was holding open the passenger door.

"Well, come on, 007, I haven't got all day," he said, in a voice EXACTLY like Q's.

REALLY LATE, SATURDAY NIGHT: WAY PAST BARRY'S NORMAL BEDTIME

Barry was already half-asleep by the time he got into bed. His mom tucked him in while his dad stood by. It had been a long time since *both* his parents had put him to bed—but then it had been a big day. It had been a big week.

Barry stretched out, luxuriating in being back in his own bed. As he did so, his hand went under the pillow, like it always did.

"Mom? Dad?"

"Yes?" they said together softly.

"There was a bit of paper under the pillow . . ."

Geoff frowned. But Susan said: "Oh yes! Sorry. I was cleaning your room—it didn't really need cleaning, but I wanted . . . you know . . . to keep cleaning it. I did it every day while you were in the hospital just in case, and . . . Anyway, yesterday I was airing your sheets out and this bit of paper— with some writing on it?—flew up from underneath the pillow and out of the window. I tried to grab it, but couldn't. Sorry, darling. Was it important?"

Barry shook his head and smiled. "No," he said. "Not important at all." And let his head drop back on to the pillow.

He saw his parents smile at each other. Then, he said one more thing. Very quietly. Very sleepily.

"This has been the best birthday I've ever had," he said. "And you are the best parents in the world . . ."

For a moment, it looked like his mom might cry.

Which would have meant quite a lot of tears as his dad *was* already crying. But also smiling. At the same time.

"Thank you, Barry," he said.

"Yes, thank you," said his mom, coming back to kiss him once more on the forehead. "Now get some sleep . . . ."

"I will," he said.

They went out and shut the door.

As they did so, the room began to shake. The shaking stirred Barry. He opened his eyes and thought he saw something.

It may have been a trick of the light washing across the wall from the truck trundling down the A41 outside. But on the far wall his poster of Lionel Messi seemed to do a thumbs-up; and he could *swear* that James Bond raised his eyebrow . . . just a little.

Acknowledgments

I'd like to thank, for all their various amazing and invaluable work toward the creation of this book, Geraldine Stroud, Elorine Grant, Kate Clarke, Samantha Swinnerton, Georgia Garrett, and Nick Lake. I'd particularly like to thank Ann-Janine Murtagh for her untiring positivity about, and passion for, the whole project, without which I very much doubt it would have happened. Closer to home, thanks must go, as ever, to Morwenna Banks, without whose support I'm not sure I'd do anything at all.